"You Shouldn't Have Followed Me,"

she said. "It should have been obvious, even to you, that I wanted to be alone."

"It's all the old hate and resentment, building up for years and years," he said, his voice low. "And frustration. I wanted you then, you know. It drove me to distraction how much I wanted you, and I held back. And then I discovered I had been a fool. And then I wondered what it would have been like, satisfying that lust."

"Lust?" She raised her head at the fresh cut of his words. "I loved you then, Kale. I know it was just puppy love. But that's what you felt for me? Lust?"

He didn't answer her aloud, but she saw a passing frown, and his eyes strayed from her face. She saw that it might just be his pride talking, for he wasn't going to admit he loved her once...if he ever had.

Dear Reader,

Merry Christmas from Silhouette Desire—where you're guaranteed powerful, passionate and provocative love stories that feature rugged heroes and spirited heroines who experience the full emotional intensity of falling in love!

The always-wonderful Cait London is back with this December's MAN OF THE MONTH, who happens to be one of THE BLAYLOCKS. In *Typical Male,* a modern warrior hero is attracted to the woman who wants to destroy him.

The thrilling Desire miniseries TEXAS CATTLEMAN'S CLUB concludes with *Lone Star Prince* by Cindy Gerard. Her Royal Princess Anna von Oberland finally reunites with the dashing attorney Gregory Hunt who fathered her child years ago.

Talented Ashley Summers returns to Desire with *That Loving Touch,* where a pregnant woman becomes snowbound with a sexy executive in his cabin. The ever-popular BACHELOR BATTALION gets into the holiday spirit with *Marine under the Mistletoe* by Maureen Child. *Star-Crossed Lovers* is a Romeo-and-Juliet-with-a-happy-ending story by Zena Valentine. And an honorable cowboy demands the woman pregnant with his child marry him in Christy Lockhart's *The Cowboy's Christmas Baby.*

Each and every month, Silhouette Desire offers you six exhilarating journeys into the seductive world of romance. So make a commitment to sensual love and treat yourself to all six for some great holiday reading this month!

Enjoy!

Joan Marlow Golan
Senior Editor, Silhouette Desire

Please address questions and book requests to:
Silhouette Reader Service
U.S.: 3010 Walden Ave., P.O. Box 1325, Buffalo, NY 14269
Canadian: P.O. Box 609, Fort Erie, Ont. L2A 5X3

Star-Crossed Lovers
ZENA VALENTINE

Silhouette® Desire®

Published by Silhouette Books

America's Publisher of Contemporary Romance

This one is for Don.

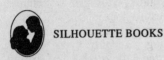 SILHOUETTE BOOKS

ISBN 0-373-76259-3

STAR-CROSSED LOVERS

This edition published by arrangement with Harlequin Books S.A.

® and TM are trademarks of Harlequin Books S.A., used under license. Trademarks indicated with ® are registered in the United States Patent and Trademark Office, the Canadian Trade Marks Office and in other countries.

Visit us at www.romance.net

Printed in U.S.A.

Books by Zena Valentine

Silhouette Desire

Star-Crossed Lovers #1259

Silhouette Romance

From Humbug to Holiday Bride #1269

ZENA VALENTINE

has had a career goal since childhood to "have adventures." Throughout her adventures in journalism, cosmetics, construction, parenting, corporate financial relations, photography, sports car racing, gardening, flying, cooking and real estate, she has carried a lifelong love of writing. She likens writing a romance novel to restarting an airplane at five thousand feet ("exciting"). Nowadays she divides her time between the north woods of Minnesota and the desert country of Nevada. Her journalist daughter and musician son are off having their own adventures.

One

Jessica Caldwell Morris felt a furious charge shoot through her chest when she looked up from her desk and saw the glazed white body of a twin-engine prop plane settle onto the runway like a giant porcelain bird.

Noble Engineering, said the crisp blue lettering on the fuselage.

It was several moments before she realized she had ceased breathing as she followed from her second-floor viewpoint the plane's slackening progress to the end of the runway. While the pilot braked, the plane slowed smoothly as if harnessed by an invisible hand, nearly stopping before it pivoted toward the fuel pumps.

A random gas stop?

Jessi hoped so.

An accident of fate?

Surely the Nobles had no business in Kenross.

"Oh God, oh God, oh God," she gasped, covering her face with her hands. She felt the sweat and the foreboding of bad memories being jarred awake. Very bad memories. Twelve-year-old very bad memories.

Thank God Chaz was down in the lounge and could take care of whoever was in the plane. Certainly there wasn't a Noble in the plane, or surely it wouldn't have stopped.

Unless they didn't know a Caldwell owned the base.

But how could they know it was her operation? Her name was Morris now, and the sign said Kenross Aviation. On the maps it was identified as Kenross Airport, although she owned the runway and all the land, buildings, equipment and individual businesses, including the repair service, new sales, flight school, plane and hangar rentals. She even owned the helicopter.

She was momentarily stunned by the plane pulling to a halt at the gas pumps. She saw Chaz's lanky form already trotting along the sidewalk onto the tarmac.

The prop slowed and abruptly stopped with a little backward jerk, and both doors flew open. The pilot remained in his seat, leaning out and flexing his shoulders as he talked to Chaz on the ground.

Her eyes darted to the other door, where she spotted the top of a man's head, hair as black and straight as crow's feathers, his body leaping with lithe grace onto the tarmac. He turned to swing the door shut, and she saw his face.

Kale Noble.

"Oh, God, no," she whispered to the empty office, clutching her clammy palms together. Even though he had been a nineteen-year-old kid and it had been twelve years, she recognized him immediately. The thin rawboned high school athlete had matured into a muscular, broad-shouldered man, his face no longer long and bony, but filled out and solid. The eyebrows that had looked as misplaced as overgrown caterpillars in his youth now blended into a face harshly handsome.

He moved with the same athletic control she remembered, although he was no longer a skinny kid. He moved faster, aggressively, with a power she sensed was born of anger and impatience.

He strode around the back of the plane with long strides, carrying a fat mahogany-colored briefcase, and he interrupted Chaz, who was climbing the short stepladder to put gas in the starboard wing tank.

Chaz nodded and retreated, replaced the gas nozzle at the pump, and jogged after Kale into the office door below her second-floor window.

He was straight and sleek, Kale was, with a flat belly and narrow hips. He wore dark pants and a short-sleeve white shirt, open at the neck in an understandable effort to cope with the hot humid June weather. He looked busy and important. Intimidating. He advanced to the office door as if he might squash anything in his way.

What was he doing here?

Please, she prayed, let his visit be brief, whatever its purpose. He was downstairs, directly below her desk. Jessi pressed her eyes closed and listened to her own breathing, jagged and starkly hollow. She felt ages-old guilt, although she knew she'd had no deliberate fault in the tragedy that had sent his brother Paul to the grave, split their families, and sent her older sister Charlotte into hell, where she had flailed through her days as if she were drowning until her death last year.

The memories came alive, overwhelming her in a blighted cloud. Eyes closed, she slowly lowered her arms, grasping her forearms. Kale had never ceased haunting her, though in recent years she'd had blessedly extended periods of relief.

Why now?

Things were going well.

She was recovering gradually from the deaths of her husband, her sister and her brother-in-law in the same plane crash a year ago, feeling good about the healing progress her niece Amanda was making, satisfied with the profits and the volume of her business, and, as always, enjoying the hours she managed to spend flying.

And now she was assailed not just by memories. It was the nightmare of Kale Noble at nineteen, a year after Paul's tragic accident, furious, in a barely controlled rage, pointing a finger at Jessi, calling her and a married Charlotte the Jezebel sisters, depraved women who caused destruction and loss to the men they so callously used and misled. And around him were familiar people, people they had known most of their lives, agreeing with him.

It wasn't until Jessi had married Rollie Morris, a distant cousin of Charlotte's husband, Frank, three years later and slept every night with her cheek against his warm body that she began to shed the nightmares and sleep through the long nights. The nightmares had not been from her imagination, but memories of a stark and nasty reality.

She focused again on the sunlit scene below. Kale's powerful strides were taking him from the office to the rental car in the parking lot, and Chaz was once again setting up to gas the aircraft. The pilot was wandering in wide circles, stretching his legs and arms, looking over the buildings, the hedge, the parking lot, the hangars, the other planes parked on the visitors' strip at perfect angles with chocks behind their wheels.

Kale backed up the rental car and drove through the parking lot to the highway.

Then, he was out of sight, leaving only a faint trail of dust through the hard gravel. Her eyes returned to Chaz who was in conversation with the pilot, pointing toward the restaurant across the parking lot.

She waited. Eventually, the pilot moved the plane to the guest parking area, kicked the pitted white chocks against the tires, and ambled lazily toward the restaurant. Chaz returned to the office downstairs.

She heard him tripping up the steps.

He stopped at the top. When she turned toward him, he was leaning his sinewy frame against the door casing, his arms folded across his chest. Sweat had stained his blue shirt under the arms and down the middle of his chest.

"So who the hell is Kale Noble?" he demanded as if he had a right to know.

She inhaled deeply and wondered what to say. A man who hates the Caldwells? A man still full of resentment for something that happened over a dozen years ago?

A bright, beautiful boy she'd thought she would love forever when she was a naive young girl?

She wondered if Kale had known it was her flying service when he landed here. Obviously, *something* had been said downstairs to inspire the accusation in Chaz's voice.

"Then he knows I'm here," she ventured. "Does he know I'm the owner?"

"He does now," Chaz said pointedly, raising an eyebrow.

She swallowed hard. "What did he say?"

"About you? Nothing. It was the way he didn't say it that set bells to ringing."

She looked out the window. "Tell me what he said, or didn't say," she commanded quietly.

"You tell me who he is," Chaz barked in reply, pushing himself away from the door frame and coming to the desk, where he placed his palms flat and leaned over to put himself within her view.

She lowered her eyes to the desktop. "Someone from the past. A reminder of a family tragedy."

"You mean the car accident that made Charlotte bonkers?"

She turned on him swiftly. "Charlotte was not bonkers," she snapped. "And I want to know what Kale Noble said to you. His brother died in that accident and none of us has been the same since. I want to know exactly what he said, or didn't say, and how he did or didn't say it."

She glared at him.

He withered. "He was looking around while I made out the rental car form, and he saw the picture on the wall of you and

Rollie when Rollie gave you your wings. I noticed he was staring at it. He asked me who you were.''

Ah, yes, the color photo Rollie had enlarged to 11x17 and framed with "Congratulations, Jessi" screaming from its plaque. It was still displayed where he had hung it nearly ten years ago, like an eyesore, she thought, but so endearingly placed she couldn't bear to remove it.

Kale wouldn't know that Rollie was her late husband, unless Chaz had told him.

Chaz continued, "I said 'the boss lady.' He said, 'it figures.' If looks could burn, that photograph of you and Rollie would be ashes.''

As if in afterthought, Chaz added, "I told him about Rollie's plane going down. And about your sister.''

So Kale knew she was a widow, and that Charlotte was dead. "And what did you find out about him?''

"President of Noble Engineering. They designed the Point Six bridge across the swamp.''

She lowered her face and rubbed her forehead. Damn! It meant he would be a fixture around Kenross for a while, maybe months. Why hadn't she noticed his company name before this?

The bridge had been in the news for the last couple of years. It was an experiment in road building to preserve the environment. Purportedly, the bridge was of a revolutionary design, the first of its kind. Why hadn't she noticed his name before? Or seen him?

All these years he had simply been a hundred and fifty miles away in Minneapolis.

"They just bought it," he said, eyeing the plane. "The boss decided he was wasting too much time on the highway.''

"I suppose I can manage to keep out of his sight," she murmured.

"What's he got against you? Charlotte was driving the car," he said.

"There's more to it than that, Chaz. It got very messy.''

She looked up at him, understanding but resenting his morbid curiosity. "Both our families got involved."

He didn't move.

"That's all, Chaz," she told him.

"Hell, I've been hearing about 'Charlotte's accident' since before she married Frank. Every time she got tanked up or did something crazy, people said it was because she caused some guy to die in a car accident. Nobody ever knew the details. Nobody dared to ask you or Charlotte about it. Sounds to me like there was a lot more to it than just a car accident and some guy ending up dead."

"It got complicated," she replied, flinching at his insensitive rendition. "But it was a long time ago, and I certainly don't want to talk about it now. How long is he using the car?"

"He's at a special city council meeting. Coupla' hours or so."

She looked out to see her twelve-year-old niece Amanda walking across the parking lot from the highway, kicking stones with the toes of her battered Nikes, her backpack flung over one shoulder. She looked a lot like Charlotte used to look, except she had a stockier build, bigger bones, and an oval face. Still, she reminded Jessi of Charlotte years ago, when she walked, lost in thought, absently kicking stones in front of her.

"Here comes Amanda," she said.

Chaz glanced at his watch. "Right on time," he replied. "What's she doing today?"

"Mowing around the east hangars," she said. "Will you help her get the mower out of the shed?"

"Sure thing," he replied and moved to the doorway.

She was relieved when he disappeared down the stairs. She refused to share something so painful and intensely personal with Chaz, who had been a part of the airport for most of his thirty-five years, an employee of Rollie's since he was twenty, and now her chief pilot.

Jessi had accumulated a wealth of knowledge over the last

year, not the least of which was that she was capable of running the business she had inherited when Rollie died. He had trained her well by encouraging her to take on responsibility a little at a time, gradually teaching her nearly everything she needed to know, as if sensing he wouldn't be around forever.

Forever? He had only lived to forty-six. And at twenty-eight, she was now the boss.

She missed Rollie, for even though their relationship had lacked intimacy and passion, he had become her best friend over the years. It had been so sudden. Rollie, Frank and Charlotte had taken the float plane on a fishing trip and crashed at a remote lake in Canada. In seconds they were all three gone, the plane sunken into several feet of mud at the bottom of a lake without a name. It had taken days to find them and bring them out.

It had been a catastrophic loss for Amanda, Chaz and Jessi. Jessi had lost her husband, her sister and her brother-in-law; Amanda had lost both her parents; Chaz had lost lifelong friends. They had been close, their lives revolving around the airfield.

But the tragedy had left Jessi little time for mourning. The business wasn't something she could set aside even for a short time in the name of grief. You didn't shut down the only paved runway in a sixty-mile radius, or ignore the growing dependence of local industry on the air traffic she provided. A new part-time pilot was needed immediately. And Frank and Charlotte's house had to be sold, and the money placed in a trust for Amanda, who now lived with her full-time.

It hadn't been a major move for Amanda, considering Charlotte had often enlisted Jessi's help with her daughter, and so Amanda already felt at home in Jessi's cottage in the trees. Amanda had had her own bedroom in the cottage since she was three years old.

Amanda settled in, though, initially in silent bitterness and depression, but eventually responding to the nurturing and love Jessi showered on her.

Jessi was thankful that Amanda loved airplanes and flying and wanted to spend her time where her father had spent his waking hours. Her niece was gradually healing.

She heard Amanda's heavy sneakers stomping up the stairs, and she turned her chair, rose to her feet and swept her arms wide to pull the hot, disheveled twelve-year-old into a long embrace. It was a ritual, and it seemed to offer as much comfort to the child as it did to the woman, for Jessi rocked her for several minutes while Amanda blurted out things that she had experienced during the afternoon at her summer school computer class. And when they'd had their afternoon fix, Amanda set her backpack on the chair by the file cabinet and looked out the windows on all four sides, checking out the field, the hangars and the restaurant across the parking lot.

"Whose twin engine?" she asked, studying the Noble plane.

"Engineering business in Minneapolis," Jessi replied. "They're designing the Point Six bridge."

Amanda's eyes flew to the parking lot. "And renting the car?"

"And the pilot's having a late lunch," Jessi added. Amanda didn't miss much.

"What am I doing today?" she asked.

"Mowing by the east hangars? Chaz will get the mower out."

"Good. I like that," Amanda said. "Pelly's doing a 500 on Oliver's new plane. I want to stop by and watch." There didn't seem to be any part of the aviation business Amanda wasn't interested in, even a routine 500-mile inspection by Pelly, Kenross's only aviation mechanic.

"Have at it," Jessi said, grinning.

Amanda gave her a quick kiss on the cheek and trotted down the steps. Jessi watched her retreating back, tendrils of warm feelings twining through her chest. Amanda plodded in from the summer school bus every day as if each step were an effort, and dragged herself to wherever Jessi happened to be, and then she threw herself against her aunt and sucked in the love, surveyed the place she loved best on earth and, revived, usually bounced to do whatever job had been assigned to her for that day.

Even at her tender age, Amanda had a sophisticated knowledge about airplanes, and she was capable of flying a single prop, though she would not be able to solo legally until she was sixteen.

Jessi confined herself to her office until Chaz left to give lessons, and then she moved down to the counter, for it was the busiest time of day in late afternoon when the weather was good and people came off their jobs to take lessons or simply fly around the area.

There was a lull about six o'clock and she wandered through the lounge to look for Amanda across the field among the east hangars. Jessi stood at the windows, aware suddenly that the door had opened and closed. When she turned, she was staring at Kale Noble as tense and as beautiful as a classical Roman statue, still and straight, errant strands of black hair slashing over his forehead, eyes so dark the pupils were lost in them, his jaw tight, making him look even more rugged up close than he had from the second floor.

If he smiles, his face will crack like dry clay, she thought, although even if he never smiled she would still think him the best-looking man she had ever known.

Her heart raced as a charge of something hot jolted from her scalp to her socks and she wondered what he would say, or do. She hoped he would not attack with sharp words. She wanted to be polite, to say hello, but she envisioned him turning even that into some kind of evil suggestion and slamming her greeting, whatever it might be, with clever sarcasm.

And so she said nothing, but she stared at him across the lounge. He responded by raising an eyebrow, a facial gesture he had obviously perfected in the last decade or so.

''Hello, Jessi,'' he said. It seemed more a challenge than a greeting.

She tried twice to speak and on the second try said, "Hello, Kale."

He pulled a key from his pocket and flung it to the side with casual accuracy so that it landed on the countertop. "I brought your car back."

"Yes," she murmured, her insides churning with uncommon wildness. "I kind of figured that you had."

He was very still as he studied her, then he quietly offered belated condolences on losing her sister and her husband, after which she thanked him.

His face was unreadable. "Nice place," he said. "Imagine my surprise to find you here."

She moved toward him, knees trembling and palms sweating. There were forms to be completed and signed now that he had returned the car. She walked up to him and faced him and saw the fine lines in his skin, too many for a man who was only thirty-one. She wanted to reach up and brush aside the strands of hair that had broken loose from where they were supposed to be, but, of course, she would never do that, not when everything about him screamed "forbidden."

She brushed past him and slipped behind the counter, found the form, completed the last few blanks, signed it, and pushed it across the counter with the pen. He turned, picked up the pen with long tanned fingers and signed it.

"Imagine *my* surprise to see your company plane landing here," she said, watching his tanned hands, one holding the pen, the other holding down the form. "Your business must be doing well."

"Extremely well," he said, tearing off the back sheet. "We have projects in several states."

She transferred the amount due to his credit card charge, adding it to the gas charge, then totaling, adding tax, before pushing it toward him to sign.

"Congratulations on your success," she said. "How are your parents? Has your father retired?"

He signed the second form. Then she tore off his copy and

stapled it to the car rental form. He looked up. "My father barely recognizes me, and my mother's life is hell, trying to take care of him. I'll tell her you inquired."

She abruptly stopped, feeling guilt. "I'm sorry," she told him softly. "It must be difficult." She remembered that Matthew Noble had withdrawn into a shell of grief after the accident and Regina had been desperate to rescue him. Apparently, her efforts had failed.

Kale's eyes narrowed, his hostility barely harnessed. "Difficult?" It was a scoff. "You can't imagine what 'difficult' has meant to my family over the years."

She watched him walk toward the door, watched him hesitate and then stop and look at her. "So you own all this now. The whole thing. Airport, flight service, restaurant."

"Not the restaurant," she corrected, hating the huskiness in her voice.

"Well, I'm sure you know how to get that if you want it," he said, his voice low and hard. "See you next trip, Jessi Caldwell," he added as he walked away.

"It's Morris!" she called after him. "It's Jessi Morris now!"

"Don't I know it," he answered quietly. Then he was gone.

She banished the guilt. She had no reason to feel responsible in the tragedy that had torn apart both their families. She had not played the Jezebel, as he thought.

She had simply been in love, and suffocating in a mire of good intentions gone bad.

She didn't blame him for his resentment, however. She had been an innocent sixteen-year-old too shocked and hurt to defend herself against his accusations. When anger had set in at his perceived betrayal, she had fled without explanation.

And now it was too late by at least a dozen years.

At last report there hadn't yet been a single successful attempt at turning back the clock to replay the past with a revised script. Regrettable, she thought, feeling again the old sharp pain, for she would have done quite a few things differently if given a second chance.

Two

Kale Noble looked out the window of the Bonanza as Phil Bergerson lifted the twin-engine craft expertly off the runway. He watched the line of tidy hangars race by in a blur, and then he looked back at the two-story building, the second floor with dark-tinted windows on all four sides, resembling a sprawling, oversize control tower.

It was a prosperous fixed-base operation and it belonged to Jessi Caldwell. If he'd known, he might have thought twice about bidding on the Point Six. Hell, the project was going to be a pain in the posterior anyway, without having to deal with one of the Jezebel sisters. He should have his brain examined for taking on a revolutionary design that, if there were significant flaws, could ruin his business.

He looked down as the plane swung to the left into the flight pattern at the end of the runway, and then left again. He heard the gear retracting, and he saw the field and the buildings from the air once more before they angled away.

She must be a wealthy woman, he thought, and all she'd

had to do was sleep with an old guy named Rollie Morris, then marry him and wait for him to die. It was what he'd come to expect from a Caldwell.

It was the anger, he told himself for the twentieth time that afternoon; it was the anger that was making his blood race.

She had changed. He could see that right away. She had matured well into a softly rounded woman. There was something luscious about her, even in her khaki shorts and military-style shirt. It was a masculine outfit, but the belt nipped in her waist and left no doubt she was a woman with nicely pert breasts and rounded hips.

She still had big brown eyes—fawn eyes, he used to call them—and baby doll cheeks with dimples so deep when she smiled, a full wide mouth and sandy blond hair that frizzed and curled with unruly defiance. He wondered whether she was still soft-spoken, or whether her bent toward deceit and manipulation had let her true character show itself.

Hell, she'd only been fifteen at the time of the accident, and sixteen the last time he saw her, after their blowup. He had been ashamed because he'd fallen for her phony innocence and her soft touch. But it was his first time in love and he would have given her anything. It was when he learned only a fool trusted a female, and he had been the worst kind of fool.

It had cost him, learning that lesson, just as it had cost his parents. But Paul had paid the ultimate price.

And the Caldwell sisters had sailed blithely out of their lives with no consequences, anxious to be Up North by their Fancy Acres summer retreat, now that they had both found better "catches" than the Nobles. Kale tried not to think about *when* Rollie Morris had caught Jessi's attention.

He had smarted for a long time from humiliation, and he experienced a peculiar, lasting pain very high in his gut, very close to his heart.

She was the first girl he had ever kissed.

Why had he thought of that when he saw her, silhouetted

against the window in the base lounge? Why had he remembered that she had swept his breath away when he kissed her? Why, when she came close to him and faced him, did he remember how his randy teenage body had ached for her, how he had denied himself even touching her because he thought she was too innocent and precious, and he wanted to marry her someday when they grew up?

But when she went about her business there at the base, efficiently filling out the forms, he remembered how she had, at such a tender age, sweetly deceived him about a number of things that were important to him.

It was anger, he told himself again, that made his body feel as though he had been running a great distance; his pulse pounded in his ears, and he felt the sweat running down the middle of his back in spite of the cool air in the plane. And a crazy kind of anger it was, because it stirred his groin and left him with an insane inclination to pull Jessi by the hair until she was so close to him he could imprison her with his body. And then what? Ravish her? Make love to her?

He didn't know. It had hit him like a blow from an unseen assailant. He hadn't seen it coming. It had happened when he saw her, when she walked to him, and brushed past him and coolly took care of his paperwork at the counter. He didn't want her, he told himself. It wasn't desire or attraction. It was some crazy manifestation of the resentment he had harbored all these years.

It was unhealthy to think about Jessi Caldwell.

He could recognize that plain enough.

Hell, he had finally come to terms with his destructive prejudice about women, and had finally let himself envision having a wife. He thought of Londa, quiet, intellectual and reliable, and he thought of the diamond he had *almost* given her.

Well, she hadn't turned out to be the right one, but he knew it was what he wanted, a wife and children.

There was certainly no room in his life for a troublemaker like Jessi Caldwell.

* * *

Jessi overheard the conversation when two weeks later Kale flew in and the rental car was already in use. With a certain chiding enjoyment Chaz officiously said he was sorry, "but Kenross Aviation cannot legally provide customer transportation when the rental car is not available."

Annoyed with Chaz's attitude, Jessi wiped her suddenly sweaty palms on her cotton slacks, strolled into the room where Kale was now on the telephone with the bridge contractor. Kale said, "If you can get me to the contractor's office in the industrial park, I can handle it."

He froze when he saw her. She saw him stop talking, stop moving, stop breathing, and she wondered what was going on in his head.

"I'll drive you," she said, and found her voice so strangled she wasn't sure he had heard her. It was several long seconds before he ceased staring at her and spoke again into the phone.

"I'll be there shortly," he said, and hung up the telephone, returning his hard, cold gaze to her.

She walked past him to the door, past a stunned Chaz, and didn't look back, assuming Kale was following her. When she was through the sidewalk gate, he drew alongside her.

"Why?" he demanded.

"It's good business," she said.

"But it's my business. It's Noble Engineering."

"You're a customer," she replied.

She opened the door of her sports car, her one concession to luxury, her submission to Amanda's pressure to buy a "black sports job with lotsa chrome." She expected it to bring derision from Kale, but she was in the driver's seat this time and he was, temporarily at least, dependent upon her good will.

"Did it come with the business?"

"No."

"Good taste."

"Thank you."

"Do you know where to take me?"

"Yes."

"How do you know where I'm going?"

"I know where my customers go when they come to town. It's good business," she reminded him again with deceptive confidence.

"It could be a problem, your rental car not being available when I need it," he said harshly.

"Call ahead and it will be there." She made an effort to keep her tone pleasant, treating him as a valued customer.

"Next time."

She reached in her pocket and pulled out two business cards. "Here. For you, and for your secretary."

In her peripheral vision she saw him look at the cards and then put them in the breast pocket of his shirt. "Advice taken," he said.

She drove in silence until they came to the industrial park. At Kale's direction, she turned left toward the temporary head-quarters of Burness Contracting. The company had moved in several months ago when it began constructing the bridge. Curt Burness was a regular customer at Kenross Aviation; he rented one of her large hangars for his company plane.

"If I had a smaller plane, I could land at a private field near here," Kale said as she was pulling into the Burness yard.

"Your choice. I can sell you a smaller plane," she said.

He snorted a short, humorless laugh.

She stopped the car and he opened the door. "You have a damn monopoly. The nearest decent airport is sixty miles away," he said.

Jessi forced a cold smug smile. "Yes, and I hope to keep it that way."

"Thanks for the ride," he said and slammed the door.

As she drove away, she looked in the rearview mirror and saw that he stood in the parking lot and watched her car until she turned out of view.

She wondered whether he was married, had a family. What

had his life been like? His father had apparently never recovered his senses and Kale had obviously taken over the presidency of the company. She wanted to ask about Reggie Mom, his mother, and how her health was, but she was afraid of what that might stir up, afraid of an explosion, really, and she wouldn't blame him.

She understood now why he hated her. It made perfect sense that he should hate the Caldwell sisters, and it gave her a sickening feeling, even though she had not intended to hurt him, that he had reason to blame her.

Back then, she had fostered a growing resentment because she thought his accusations were unfounded and unfair, as if he was sick of her and grasping for excuses to drive her out of his life. She had resented him for most of the last twelve years.

It was Charlotte's posthumous letter, left years earlier with Frank's attorney, that finally revealed just how heinous the Caldwell crimes against the Nobles had been. Jessi had been the pawn in a game she hadn't understood.

She had been sixteen years old, in love and incredibly naive, trying to keep her family from shattering, trying to be the good daughter.

The Nobles had suffered a terrible loss, and Charlotte had done a despicable thing to Paul. Not only had she driven recklessly after drinking, but she had in her panic abandoned him in the car at the bottom of the lake.

Everyone knew she was a good swimmer. But she hadn't gone back for him.

And all these years later, the Nobles still didn't realize just how much they had lost. They had never learned that Charlotte had kept a most precious secret from them.

As a torrid July arrived, Kale Noble became a fixture in Jessi's life, flying to Kenross weekly and calling ahead for the car. They occasionally spoke to each other, but mostly, it seemed, they glared at each other. Chaz said an unlit match held between them would burst into flames.

One afternoon, Amanda was at the counter when Kale returned from an afternoon at the bridge. As soon as Jessi realized it, she rushed to relieve Amanda to send her niece elsewhere on an errand. Anything to get Amanda out of Kale's sight.

"No!" Amanda protested. "Let me do it. I want to learn all the forms!"

"Some other time," Jessi said softly. "Not now."

"Now!" Amanda insisted.

"A little young to be working here, aren't you?" Kale muttered to the insistent girl.

She showered him with a glowing smile and thrust her hand at him in an eager greeting. "I'm Amanda Morris. I'm twelve, and I'm going to be a pilot as soon as I'm old enough to get a license."

He shook her hand and grinned. His face did not crack when he grinned, Jessi noted, but did marvelous things. His eyes sparkled, his smile nearly dazzled her. He was what Amanda would call drop-dead gorgeous when he smiled.

"My dad was a pilot," she said. "He died last summer."

Jessi heard the faint catch in her voice, but Amanda handled it well. She was only beginning to talk about her parents' untimely deaths. Jessi put a hand on her shoulder and squeezed.

The gesture was not lost on Kale, who said, "I'm sorry, Amanda, for your loss."

She looked up and gave him a painful grin of acknowledgment, and then turned to Jessi to help her fill out the form.

As Kale was signing the slip, he asked, "How old did you say you were, Amanda?"

"Twelve," she replied.

"You have the look of a Caldwell," he said. Jessi tried not to cringe at his probing.

"Of course. My mom's fault. I look totally like a Caldwell. I don't look anything like my dad," she said, tearing off the credit card flimsy and handing it to him.

"I see," he said, studying her face and then turning his dark, flashing eyes onto Jessi. "And which Caldwell sister is your mother?" he asked quietly, suggestively.

Jessi's spit caught in her throat and she coughed in a spasm. The question terrified her. Fear of discovery bit her sharply. "Kale is an old friend, Amanda, and his pilot is waiting for him. Now, get your books."

Amanda dashed for her books because it meant they were leaving and would soon eat. It was what Jessi had counted on. She forced a smile at Kale who was studying her thoughtfully.

Suddenly, he set down the briefcase and came swiftly around the counter, moving with an unreal speed. He pushed her against the cabinet behind the counter, and one hand slid into her hair, grasping it, forcing her head back. "Did you have a baby twelve years ago, Jessi?" he rasped in a voice so whispery hoarse she'd not have recognized it if he hadn't been in her face.

She felt the length of him pressed against her, felt the heat of his body through his clothes, felt helpless with her head tilted so that his face was only inches from hers and her breasts pressed against his chest.

"Did you?" he demanded, shaking her head with his skillfully painless grasp on her hair.

"If I did, Kale Noble, it certainly wasn't yours, now, was it?" she retorted, regretting that her words came out in a whisper instead of the taunting condescension she was aiming for.

The darkness in his eyes seemed to spread over his face, and the anger became a kind of grimace of pain. His face moved closer to hers, and his lips were almost touching hers when he softly blew his words into her mouth. "You lied. And you cheated. I could have..." Then he backed up abruptly and released her hair and strode to the door. He flung it open, stopped, and inhaled raggedly. "Damn you, Jessi Caldwell," he rasped and was out the door.

She buried her face in her hands and called out weakly, "It's Jessi Morris. Morris!"

In near panic, she wondered what he saw when he looked at Amanda. Certainly he wouldn't notice the distinctive Noble hairline with the widow's peak in the middle of the forehead, or the vaguely square shape of her jaw so like the Noble boys. No, he seemed to have missed that. What he saw were Jessi's fawn brown eyes and dimples and puffy lips.

He thought Amanda was *her* daughter, and that Jessi had been with another man when she was telling him she loved him, and she had let that other man do what Kale was using all his idealistic self-discipline not to do to her. He actually thought she…but, no, he would figure it out. He would know she couldn't have deceived him about having a child. They had been seeing each other while Charlotte was pregnant, although he hadn't known about the baby. He would certainly figure out that Amanda couldn't be Jessi's. He wouldn't know, of course, that Jessi having a baby was an impossibility in any case.

But when he figured out that Amanda was Charlotte's, he might also realize that she had been pregnant at the time of the accident. He was going to learn that Amanda was Paul Noble's daughter, the only grandchild in her generation, and she had been kept from the Nobles deliberately, legally claimed by the man Amanda thought had fathered her.

Jessi had thought until a year ago that Charlotte's husband, Frank, was Amanda's father. As a teen, Jessi had been appalled by her mistaken notion that Charlotte had gotten pregnant by Frank when she was talking marriage with Paul Noble.

If Jessi had been more mature and wise, she might have put the pieces together. After all, Charlotte had run off within days of the accident to marry Frank, a man she had met years earlier at Fancy Acres Resort, but had never considered more than a distant admirer. And to settle in Kenross, which she had never liked. And then to have a baby nearly two months "premature."

It was just another of a string of events that Jessi had handled badly. Even the vague suspicions that had occurred to her, she ignored, discarded, pushed aside.

Not until Charlotte's letter enlightened her did she realize the extent of the lies. Now it was a deeply personal thing, for among the truths Charlotte had admitted was that Amanda was Paul Noble's daughter.

Amanda, who was like her own child, was now in danger of being lost to her.

She didn't think she could bear to give her up if the Nobles should claim her. Amanda was the only child she would ever have.

Perhaps it had been foolish to be coy with Kale. It had just been too frightening at the moment to admit that Amanda was Charlotte's and Paul's.

And yet, she hadn't been prepared for how painful it had been to be the object of Kale's contempt, and to see the flash of hurt that underlay his intense rage at the Caldwell sisters.

Nor had she been prepared for the feel of his hard hot body pressed against her, the spicy male scent of him, and the awesome power he kept leashed so that he could bury his long fingers in her hair and not hurt her.

She had found the experience strangely exciting, sensing in him something savage, tempered only by what she identified as his innate elegance.

As she listened for Amanda's eager thudding down the steps and watched the Noble aircraft taxi away, she knew Kale would soon figure out the truth about Amanda's birth. She would have been wiser to be honest with him.

When he did figure out the truth, Jessi had two alternatives: she could confirm his suspicions, or she could lie and deny Paul's fatherhood.

She dreaded Kale's next visit.

Three

Kale flung open the door of the plane, pushed himself out onto the wing and leaped to the ground. Although it wasn't as hot and humid in Kenross as it had been a hundred and fifty miles south in Minneapolis, the blast of hot July air turned his skin sticky.

He slammed the door, and then he looked up at the small high-wing plane on base leg, perpendicular to the runway. Suddenly the engine stopped and the prop spun to a slow undulating roll. He almost felt the pilot's shock as one wing dipped sharply and then straightened. It looked for an instant as though it would take a nosedive.

All his senses moved to alert. He thought he was seeing an accident about to happen, but somehow the plane continued, turning to line up with the runway, gliding onto the tarmac with uncertain hops and jolts as it landed and then braked in jerking assaults.

Phil came to stand alongside him. "Don't worry," he said as though reading his boss's mind. "It's a student pilot flying dual. The instructor shut off the gas on final approach as part of the training.''

''Taking his life into his hands,'' Kale mused, still shaken but relieved.

''Her life, you mean,'' Phil said.

As the plane drew closer he saw what Phil had already noted, that Jessi sat in the instructor's seat. He wasn't prepared for the rush of anger that slammed like a torrent through him at the thought of Jessi being in a plane that was in trouble, of Jessi deliberately shutting off the engine while an unskilled novice was at the wheel, of Jessi putting her life in danger while he watched helplessly from the ground.

And then he caught himself, took a deep breath to clear such thoughts from his mind, and wiped sweat from his brow. He swung around to head for the office and the keys to the rental car. Was he crazy? What in the hell did he care if she wanted to take risks? If she was a flight instructor, she knew what she was doing. How was it that she goaded his anger so easily? It must be that she fed into his entrenched resentment, he thought. It was inconvenient as hell.

No one was behind the counter when he reached the office, so he reached into the drawer and helped himself to the keys. He had been here often enough, and he had reserved the car as usual, so he didn't feel as though he were trespassing. Looking around quickly, he saw two men smoking in the lounge, and he could hear Chaz's voice, presumably on the telephone in the next room.

As he closed the drawer with the car key in his hand, he looked up and the memory of nine days ago socked him in the gut. He was standing only inches from where he had lost control then, threaded his hand through her hair and pushed her against the cabinets with his body, angry that she might have been guilty of yet another betrayal a dozen years ago. But as he had held her imprisoned, his rage had colored into a desire so potent he had been obsessed with penetrating her through all the wrappings. He almost kissed her. He'd been only a scant inch from her lips. He'd had an overwhelming urge to take her mouth in a kiss savage enough to bruise.

In horror, he had backed away, cursed her and left, relying on instinct and habit alone to make his legs move, to carry him to the plane and to buckle himself in while Phil went over his checklist.

Strapping himself into the plane, he had been painfully aware that being close to her, touching her, had been a damning mistake, and had left him so shaken he forgot for a while what had inspired his rage in the first place. Every part of his body had been tight and hard with nerves bunched for attack, but it was the hardness in his groin and recognizing his oddly barbarian intentions while he had her in his power that had horrified him.

It had been a first, having his carnal desires violently awakened by rage. He was not, had never been, a violent man, had never forced a woman, or treated a woman roughly. Never in his life. He was appalled by violence, and had never associated it with either sex or desire.

It had frightened him. He had turned his head to face out the window so that Phil would not see his shame and turmoil, and he had held the briefcase temporarily on his lap to cover the evidence of his fierce arousal. Damn that woman for turning him into an animal!

No, that was unfair. She had done nothing to inspire his sudden insanity. It was something within himself, something dark and painful and frighteningly powerful, that had blossomed without warning and overshadowed his civility.

The thought that she had once wooed him with sweet shyness, and then given her body to someone else, had once again infuriated him. He had to know if that was what she had done, borne some other man's child when he as a teenager in love was lying awake nights missing her and wanting her, wondering when he might see her again. When he thought of his own young innocence and the aching need to be close to her, to take care of her and hold her and dream of a future together, he felt the ominous force of his pain-fired anger, because he had been deluded and used. He had been a fool, naive and trusting. Believing in her.

Until he heard about the "other" man and confronted her.

That Amanda might be her child had caught in his chest, until he had realized she probably wasn't Jessi's. During the return flight he had thought about that stretch of time twelve and thirteen years ago, from the accident in September to the last time he saw Jessi the following August, and he figured that if Jessi had got herself pregnant during that time, the child could not yet be twelve years old.

And then, riding in the plane alongside his pilot, he had let the other feelings overwhelm him, the ones he could neither understand nor explain that caught him in their grip when he touched her and felt the length of her soft body against him, and it sickened him. What had possessed him to handle her so harshly and to find himself wanting to force her to his will? What ill-conceived demon had driven him to such lengths?

Was it because he had harbored and nurtured his resentment toward her for so many years that when he finally found himself in her presence he could no longer contain his anger?

He was a man of infinite control. Ask anyone who knew him, the women he had known intimately, the people he worked with, his family, his clients, anyone.

To lose control now was to face a terror, for it was something within himself that he did not recognize. And could not tolerate.

That he must harness these wild errant feelings was without question. And he must do so immediately. Furthermore, he must avoid future contact with Jessi Caldwell Morris, who seemed to bring on this unconscionable behavior.

Now, standing at the cabinet where he had manhandled her nine days ago, he yanked himself back to the present. It had happened again, losing himself in the experience of touching her and suffering the consequences.

He turned quickly from the cabinet, gripping the rental car

keys in his hand and strode outside. He was heading for the rental car when she called to him, and without thought he instantly responded.

She was running from the small plane, jogging toward him in a short sleeveless tank top that revealed too many inches of delectable flat midsection, and khaki shorts, a clipboard held against her side. Her hair was frizzed by the heat and humidity, pulled into an inadequate clasp at the back of her neck so that wildly curled tendrils framed her face. As she drew near, he saw that some of the tendrils were wet and stuck to her face.

He saw the sheen of perspiration from her forehead down her clear tanned skin to the top of her breasts. That was how he had thought she would look under him when he finally made love to her, her skin glowing with pleasure and heat while she gave herself to him.

Adolescent thoughts, he warned himself, better forgotten. It would never happen. He would never make love to a woman he despised.

But he remembered her convincing innocence and her quiet vitality. He could still hear her calling his mother "Reggie Mom," see her savoring the sour apples off the sprawling tree in the Nobles' backyard.

"Kale," she called, although she was within a few feet of where he forced himself to stand without expression. He ordered himself to be absolutely still, to express nothing, to stay in control of himself.

She studied him for a moment as though she was looking for something in his face, and then she spoke. "I want to talk to you, Kale," she said quietly, still searching his face. "Would you have time after your business today?"

"What have we to talk about?"

She inhaled sharply and winced. She ran a hand over her hair which was hopelessly wild. He watched her struggle for a reply, keeping his face cool and immobile, keeping his body still while inside a fire was raging.

"Nothing, I guess," she said in a voice so low he saw rather than heard it. "Forget it," she murmured.

He should, although he would like to talk some more about Amanda. He already knew the girl was Charlotte's and not Jessi's. And he shouldn't talk to Jessi. He shouldn't allow himself to be caught in a conversation with her, and yet, he did intend to pursue his suspicion that she was hiding something in regard to Amanda. He wanted to ask when Amanda was born. He wanted to know whether there was a possibility she was Paul's.

It seemed unlikely that even the Jezebel Caldwells could have been cruel enough to withhold all these years a precious child of Paul's. Still, he wanted to know for certain.

He was watching Jessi's knotted eyebrows, and then he looked into her eyes. Hell, it was Friday afternoon, and he wouldn't mind a cool drink before he crawled back into the plane. He tried not to think of how it would be sitting near her, watching her, sharing a drink.

"All right," he said finally. "But I don't know what time I'll be back."

"I'll be here," she said softly.

He nodded and tore himself away from her soft voice and her luscious glowing woman's body, turning swiftly to walk in the opposite direction to the rental car, letting himself through the high latched gate at the end of the sidewalk. He looked back once before he tucked himself into the car, but she was gone.

Jessi wrote her instructor's comments in the student's log-book, then gassed the plane and returned it to the hangar. She looked at the schedule for the rest of the day, what planes were reserved by whom for what time periods, and she went through message slips that had been accumulating during the day, then checked the ground school schedule to make sure that Chaz had arranged his hours to teach the Saturday morning class. She would be tied up with lessons as she usually was on Saturdays, and once again she promised herself she would hire another part-time flight instructor.

She had hired Harry, a retired airline pilot, as a part-time pilot after Rollie and Frank had died, and she had given Chaz the full-time job, but she and Chaz were the only ones qualified to instruct, and during the summer she needed another person on weekends.

Amanda skipped in from school, threw herself into Jessi's embrace and told her aunt she had been invited to spend the night at a friend's. Jessi approved of the friend and agreed to drive her there if Amanda would go home and pack a bag and come back when she was ready to go.

Before leaving to transport Amanda, she told Chaz she would be gone for fifteen minutes. "If Kale Noble comes back, ask him to wait. I'll only be a few minutes."

Both Amanda and Chaz were startled at her casual words.

"Mr. Noble? That gorgeous man who said I look like my mom?" Amanda asked.

Chaz observed, "The man can hardly stand to be in the same room with you, Jessi."

"We have something to discuss," she snapped, and headed to the door so quickly Amanda had to jerk herself around to keep up.

"I'll tell him you're busy getting into your armor," Chaz yelled after her.

When she returned, Chaz was waiting for her. "You watch out for him, Jessi," he warned.

"Well, what do you think he's going to do to me, for heaven's sake," she scoffed, fleeing further questions by dashing to her upstairs retreat.

"Jessi!" he shouted, taking the steps two at a time behind her. "Did you ever look in his eyes? They're black as coal, like there's a fire burning in there. And the way he acts like he has the whole world in his control. Curt Burness says he's a genius! A genius, for crying out loud!"

"Curt Burness said that? Interesting." She pulled an accounting book out of a desk drawer. Well, Curt Burness would know a genius if he worked with one.

Chaz was silent for a moment. She could hear his heavy breathing. When she looked up, his face was a picture of chagrin, but his voice had softened and his arms were still. "I think he could hurt you," he said.

She was dismayed not only by the intensity of his concern, but also by the unwitting accuracy of his words. Any hurt Kale Noble caused her wouldn't be of the physical variety, but rather it would be the soul-deep pain of a twice-broken heart. She forced a small smile. "Thank you for worrying, Chaz, but Kale Noble has never been a violent person," she replied, deliberately misinterpreting his prediction.

"Every time I see that damned Noble plane I get a pain in my gut. Every time I see it fly away I feel relieved. The guy is arrogant as hell," Chaz continued.

So it wasn't just her imagination that Kale Noble paced through life with an aura of power and intimidation. It wasn't just memories of the past or her awareness that he resented her that gave him an appearance almost sinister. And then, there had been the incident behind the counter the last time they were together, when he crowded her and put his hand in her hair. She saw him as a walking energy force, threatening her emotional stability with his raw sensuality.

"You're probably right, Chaz," she agreed. "I'll suggest we meet at the restaurant."

He reluctantly left, and she worked on accounts payable, stopping frequently while her mind wandered.

Was she doing the right thing intending to probe to learn how close he was to discovering the truth about Amanda's parentage? She deeply regretted her taunting and defiant response to his question when he held her against the cabinet and let her see for the first time that his rage had been fostered by abject pain. It wasn't in her nature or true to her principles that she be coy with him. She didn't approve of playing games with people's feelings. Certainly it was inappropriate not to be honest about a subject that was so emotionally charged it was bound to cause yet another series of painful eruptions between the Caldwells and the Nobles.

Still, she didn't think she could bear to tell Kale and risk losing Amanda to the Caldwells' archenemies.

Whatever action she took or didn't take in the matter, the truth might eventually be revealed now that Kale was a regular customer, and if it was, all of them were going to be hurt in some way. Better, she thought, to determine how close Kale was to figuring things out. If he should discover Paul was Amanda's father, his accusations and bitterness were likely to curdle the air. And she wouldn't blame him.

She disliked working on accounts payable, and when she caught herself writing the wrong amount on a check, she ceased her efforts, and stared out the window at the nice flurry of activity on her airfield.

In spite of the uncomfortable heat, people were coming to fly airplanes, their own that were hangared there and hers that they rented. She saw her sleek six-passenger aircraft turn from downwind to base leg and knew that Harry, her part-time pilot, was returning with officers from one of the corporations that regularly used her flight service.

There was a line of three planes at the gas pump occupying Chaz.

She put away her books and went down to the counter.

She wandered into the lounge to visit with the men who sat around because they loved flying and at the moment had nowhere to go. Sometimes there were a few women around, too, but seldom.

There was no profit in idle pilots sitting around the lounge, but Jessi encouraged it nonetheless, as Rollie had, because she liked the camaraderie. She liked to hear the old-timers talk about tail draggers and tease the younger pilots about the minimal skills required nowadays to fly "tricycles."

Being a pilot made you a part of a special fellowship. She had felt it the first time she set foot in Rollie's lounge, and she had known immediately that she wanted to be a part of it. After her first ride aloft, she recognized that a whole new world had been opened to her, a world she was born to.

At times like this she missed Rollie, whose devotion to flying and his friends had left a gaping hole in her life.

And then she felt a bite of guilt because in recent days her thoughts of Rollie had been insidiously replaced by thoughts of Kale Noble, who, as Chaz fantasized, was bedeviling her.

She grinned when he came through the door, having handed off his briefcase to Phil, and the words fell from her lips, "Well, just think about the devil and..."

He eyed her from where he stood by the counter, his white cotton shirt stained with sweat and fine splatters of mud. His black hair was blown out of its natural waves, and strands were plastered to his gleaming skin. He looked rugged and earthy, sensual and elegant.

She stared at him from the lounge. He ran a hand over his ruffled hair and headed for the rest room. When he emerged, the mud splatters were less evident, his face was clean and his hair combed.

"Does that place across the parking lot sell liquor?" he demanded.

"There's a bar," she replied.

"Good. Let's talk there," he said, reaching out a hand in an impatient gesture to have her join him. He didn't ask. He just made the decision and expected her to agree.

Well, the talk was her idea and he had reluctantly gone along with it. So let him be high-handed about choosing the site. She had intended to meet in the restaurant anyway.

They walked across the parking lot in awkward silence. She wondered again whether she was doing the right thing, or whether she should keep mum and avoid the risk of triggering further suspicions from Kale.

If her timing would prove to be bad, or if he would lose his temper again and pull her within his body force as he had

done before, she would once again find him kindling wild sensations, wrecking her inner balance.

Too late, she recognized she was only dreading the aftermath, not the experience.

Four

Kale ordered a glass of ice water followed by a martini. Jessi ordered lemonade.

"Nothing stronger?" he questioned.

"I'm on call for the chopper tonight," she explained, not telling him she rarely drank. It interfered with flying. Besides, most of it tasted like caustic medicine, she thought.

"The chopper? On call for what?"

"We have a contract for emergency air ambulance service. One of us is always on call. See?" She tapped the beeper attached to the belt of her shorts.

"So you're also qualified to fly a helicopter," he observed.

"Chaz, too. Unfortunately, we're the only two, and so one or the other of us is always on call, twenty-four hours a day, seven days a week. But we don't have many calls."

"You put in a lot of hours," he murmured, draining the glass of ice water. "So you're finding there are drawbacks to owning your own business?" He flung the words at her as though it was righteous consequence for her ambition.

"It never seems like too many. I love it," she replied.

"I feel the same way about my business. I always have, even as a teen. I couldn't wait to get through engineering school and be a real part of the company."

"I know," she said softly. "I remember." She remembered that his father hadn't been concerned about Kale's education, or where he finally found employment. Yet how fortunate he was that he had a son like Kale who could competently take over.

"I didn't expect as much responsibility as I got, though, or so soon. My father lost interest after Paul's accident. He always planned that his financial son would actually run the business when he was ready to give it up." Kale's voice was low and hard, but she heard every word, all of it familiar facts. "I would simply be chief of engineering when the Noble boys eventually took over."

He looked up at her, his eyes simmering. "There wasn't much left of the business by the time I got out of school. My father, well, he has, uh, withdrawn over the years."

She didn't know what to reply. It was all so brutal, the consequences of the accident that Charlotte had caused.

Finally, she said, "I was always fond of your father, and I was especially fond of Paul. I've thought of them both many times over the years, especially at Christmastime." Christmas Eve had always been a special time for the Caldwells and Nobles.

His lean dark face took on dramatic shadows in the dimly lit atmosphere, highlighting the rugged lines. He was not overtly accusing, but she felt the guilt nevertheless for the pain her family had caused.

"You must have dedicated much of your life to Noble Engineering for it to be the success it is," she murmured.

"Yes," he conceded in little more than a whisper. "Other things have been neglected."

"No family?"

He hesitated, staring hard into her eyes. "No wife. No children. Yet. No home in the 'burbs. I find I don't even get away on vacation often enough," he said.

"Where do you go on vacation?" she asked in a desperate attempt to get the conversation into another direction. His lack of family was none of her business, and why should she care anyway?

"The last one was with a, er, friend to the Grand Caymans. I didn't want to be gone a whole week, but once I was there, a week didn't seem long enough," he said, leaning on his elbows, looking at her steadily.

Did he see her reaction? Could he see how his words affected her, sending tiny explosions through her chest? A friend? Well, of course, it had been a woman. She hadn't seen a wedding ring and assumed he was not married, and now she knew he had never got to the altar at all. But if a woman friend traveled on vacation with him, obviously he was in a serious relationship with her, she concluded.

"I thought you would have married long ago," she murmured.

"I've been thinking about it. I would like a family."

"Well, give marriage serious consideration, Kale. I hope when it happens you'll be as happy as I was being married to Rollie." Surely he couldn't see that she was brimming with turmoil, and although she meant what she said, the words were to hide her inner distress.

He narrowed his eyes as if doubting. "Let's talk about Amanda," he said. It was not a suggestion, but was said in a low commanding voice.

"She's Charlotte's," she blurted, clutching her wet lemonade glass to steady her hands.

"I figured that out." When she didn't reply, he remarked, "I owe you an apology."

She nodded awkwardly, taken aback by his admission that he had been in the wrong. "Accepted," she said. "And I'm sorry I was so defiant and, well, vague." *And afraid.* But she didn't say that, only lowered her eyes. The feelings he generated were too strong and she didn't want him to see how shaken she was.

She could feel his eyes on her, though. She could feel his heat projecting itself, touching her, and she kept her face down, her gaze on the tall lemonade she clung to irrationally as if it might leap away from her on its own.

"You had every right to be afraid," he said quietly, as if reading her mind. Or was he used to people being afraid of him? "I lost my temper. A rare occasion."

She looked up. His eyes were still hard. Chaz was right. He was dangerous. Maybe she would do well not to think of him as the boy he had been, gentle and trusting, so loving and tender he stole her breath when he kissed her. He was a man now, and as his body had grown more powerful with maturity, so had his force of energy.

"When was she born?"

"Who?"

"Amanda. When was she born?"

"May 15," she said, swallowing hard. She knew the question would come sooner or later. Now he had what he needed to figure it all out.

He stared at her for long seconds, and she saw his mind calculating. It didn't take long. "She could be Paul's."

Her answer was a long time in coming. The conversation was not moving as she had expected. Obviously, she had underestimated him, and now it was a kind of fear she felt, and a jolt of strangeness. After having assumed Amanda was Frank's all these years, and then discovering the truth after Charlotte's death, she had never revealed it before now.

"Charlotte said Amanda was premature," she said. "She was born seven and a half months after she and Frank were married."

He folded his hands under his chin, as if he doubted her. "Nine months after Charlotte and Paul became engaged and were seeing each other every day," he added.

Jessi sipped her lemonade and nodded in silence.

"Then, Amanda is Paul's daughter, isn't she?" His voice was so low with menace, she shivered at the sound of it.

She stared at him, silently begging him to soften, not to insist, not to take Amanda away from her. Fear knocked her speechless.

"Do you deny it?" he probed.

She pursed her lips and steadfastly met his glare, shaking her head finally.

"So it's true." She saw the rage vivid and real in every feature of his face, although he barely moved and his voice remained low.

She understood the anger. In spite of having arranged this session to discover how close he was to the truth, she hadn't wanted to discuss Amanda's parentage in detail. Neither had she estimated he would already have figured it out. She could see that his venom was ages old, simmered to a high concentration.

She pushed her chair back, her intent, suddenly, to flee. "I'm sorry I brought this up. I'm sorry I thought we could discuss—" She rose abruptly.

He was up and reaching across the table, his hand on her forearm, coaxing her back into the chair. "Sit down, please."

"You can't force me to stay here," she cried, hushing her voice. "This conversation is done. You make me feel dishonorable."

"What does a Caldwell know of honor?" he returned.

"It was a mistake to try to deal with you!"

"Just what kind of deal did you have in mind?"

She hushed her voice. "Your sarcasm will get us nothing but more anger. Do you intend to rip open new wounds? Or discuss the future with...reasonableness?"

His grimace revealed the pain she didn't want to see behind his sarcasm.

This time she pushed her chair back several feet and stood beyond his reach. "You're...impossible!" she charged, and walked swiftly out of the bar, through the foyer and onto the steamy hot parking lot. She started toward the airfield, and then changed her mind when she felt tears choking her, and headed in a dead run for the trees that hid the lake and her cottage from view of restaurant patrons.

It was too hot for running, and by the time she reached the path under the trees, perspiration was running down her face and neck. She was quickly out of breath. When she reached her cottage, she ran out onto the dock with the intent of slipping into the cool water. Instead, she stood at the end of the dock, her body heaving as she sobbed and tried to catch her wind. She bent over, elbows locked, resting her hands on her knees, forcing herself to breathe in deeply through her nose and exhale through pursed lips.

She felt his weight on the dock before she heard him, and when she peered around her shoulder, he was slowly advancing on her. She quickly wiped her eyes, straightened and turned to face him, but his ominous visage intimidated her and she backed away.

He reached for her suddenly and pulled her toward him as her heel struck air at the end of the dock. She realized at that moment that he had reached out to prevent her from stepping backward into the lake.

Still, she wrestled to get away, but he pulled her against him, and as she continued to struggle, he countered her by holding her tightly against his chest, his arms all the way around her, creating a hot steel cage she had no hope of escaping.

She heard his low voice and felt his breath disturbing the curls above her temple. "Give it up, Jessi. Give it up. You can't get away from me. I'll hold you until you stop fighting me."

It was another kind of emotion that gripped her then, shocking her, burning her from the inside. She stopped fighting him, but only because something powerful within her made his chest a lover's cradle and his arms a haven.

So she gave up the struggle as she became aware of immense sensuality, hotter than the air and the sun, born of their bodies pressed together, the pressure of his solid arms and his hard chest, and gradually, from the part of him that was growing thick and heavy against her belly. Even when she stopped struggling, she did not so much relax as melt against him, against all of him, caught in arms that continued to hold her close. He was enormous against her, and she might have pulled away the lower part of her body because his arms were enfolded over her upper back.

But she didn't.

She felt herself turning liquid down low, under her shorts, and her body moved beyond her conscious intent so that her back arched and her head went back. Next she felt his lips crushing hers, and then withdrawing as though he intended to stop, but they came back again and tasted, nibbled and brushed, and when she opened to him he came into her mouth with his tongue, owning her mouth, taking as he explored, commanding with practiced tenderness.

She felt his hand slide down her back and hold her against him, and then she felt his knee smoothly work its way between her legs, forcing her left leg up. His lips slid away and trailed expert little bites down the side of her neck.

"Don't," she cried. "Kale, don't."

It was an exciting prison, and although she pleaded to be released she did not struggle. She knew she had to stop him, but her body responded to him with a passion entirely new to her, like an aphrodisiac shot into her veins to create a craving she neither understood nor fought.

"You're a witch, Jessi Caldwell," he whispered into her mouth. "You take all my discipline away." Then, he stepped back from her.

But he held her up by the shoulders, or she'd have fallen into the lake. Her equilibrium was gone, her head spinning. And something else had happened, a wetness and a clutched feeling, incredibly erotic and needy, so alive. And sensitive.

If he touched her now anywhere below the waist, she would explode.

She shook her head to clear away the sensations that rocked and confused her, new sensations, new feelings, shocking and embarrassing, leaving her feeling helpless.

"What did you do to me?" she asked, her breathing ragged.

He raised an eyebrow. "You don't know?"

Her face reddened. She felt the unwelcome flush, and she bit her lip and shook his hands off her shoulders. "Don't touch me again," she said.

"You're a hot little number, Jessi Caldwell," he told her, his mouth pulled derisively into a small accusing grin.

She looked up at him in horror and hugged her arms around herself, cringing from the possible accuracy of his words. "Oh, God," she groaned, and pressed her eyes closed and dropped her chin against her chest.

His hands came up again, and this time grasped her arms gently just below her shoulders. "I'm sorry," he said in a low voice. "Don't be misled by my momentary loss of control. I know the kind of woman I want a lasting relationship with, and it isn't you."

She inhaled in jerky installments, crushed by his insulting apology which was more to himself and a wife he didn't yet have than it was to her, as though she were the cause instead of the victim. Still, she was in no condition to protest, for her body had still not returned to normal. It felt as if it never would.

She recognized that she could not be alone with this man, for he overpowered her with his touch and left her aching for something she couldn't have imagined wanting before he gave her that wicked teasing.

"You shouldn't have followed me," she said, shaking, very slowly recovering. "It should have been obvious, even to you, that I wanted to be alone."

"It's all the old hate and resentment, building up for years and years," he said, his voice low. "And frustration. I wanted you then, you know. It drove me to distraction how much I wanted you, and I held back. And then I discovered I had been a fool. And then I wondered what it would have been like, satisfying that lust.''

''Lust?'' She raised her head at the fresh cut of his words. ''I loved you then, Kale. I know it was just puppy love. But that's what you felt for me? Lust?''

He didn't answer her aloud, but she saw a passing frown, and his eyes strayed over the lake behind her. She saw that it might just be his pride talking, for he wasn't going to admit he loved her once, if he ever had.

''I think I'm recovered now,'' she said quietly, struggling to shed the pain from his pointed jabs. ''If you'll step aside, we can get off this dock and under the shade of the trees.''

''Right,'' he agreed, and stepped aside so that she could lead the way to shore.

She stopped on the path under the trees. ''Why did you follow me?''

''Because your last words made sense,'' he said coolly, the hardness back in his dark eyes. ''This situation is going to cause enough pain. It will be easier for all of us if we can be reasonable.''

''I don't think you're capable of being reasonable,'' she said, like a wasp, she thought, making each word sting.

''Point taken. I'll try to prove you wrong.''

''Then tell me what you intend to do.''

''What do you expect? A grandchild will bring new vitality to my mother's life, and maybe a child of Paul's will even reach something in the recesses of my father's mind. Amanda will bring a sense of family to all of us. I want to know her. I want to spend time with her.''

Jessi winced, near tears. ''I can't bear the thought of giving her up.''

''She's not yours. You should have children of your own,'' he said.

''No, I can't... I never will—'' she stammered, embarrassed

beyond good sense. "Medical reasons," she muttered in her distress, despising him for forcing the admission from her.

"I'm sorry," he said curtly, looking away for a moment and then zeroing in on her eyes with his next words. "But Amanda is a Noble. We have a right to have her in our lives."

"I've had her since she was born," she protested. "Even when Charlotte was still here, I took care of her a lot of the time. It's why I didn't go to college, because Charlotte was so, so...unhappy here, and Amanda needed me. You see, I lived with Charlotte and Frank while I was in high school here. Later, when I married Rollie, I still had her a lot of the time. She's always had her own bedroom in the cottage. I discovered while I was married to Rollie she was the only child I'd ever have."

"She had two parents!" he declared. "Where in the hell was her mother all those years?"

"Charlotte...had a difficult life," she countered. "Problems. She had to, uh, leave sometimes, you know, go off by herself. But she loved Amanda. Amanda was the most important person in her life. She wanted to spare her daughter the restless symptoms of her suffering. She wanted her to have...stability. Here in Kenross. And she knew how much I loved Amanda. Charlotte did her best." They were on tricky ground and she was uncomfortable arguing for Charlotte's motherhood because the truth was something she wasn't prepared to share with him, that Paul's death had tormented her until the day she died.

"Poor Charlotte," he scoffed.

"You don't know what she went through!" she cried.

He narrowed his eyes, which were cold and very dark. She saw his jaw tighten and his body tense. "I've never forgotten what the Caldwells did to us. We were decimated as a family after the accident. Everything fell apart. It was my rage that motivated me to finish my education and take over the company before it fell into bankruptcy." He stopped to inhale deeply, and then he continued. "To finally see you again after all these years, it's like being stung all over again. I wasn't just angry at you and Charlotte, Jessi. I was equally angry at myself for being such a fool, for getting sucked in by you and your act.''

"I handled it so badly," she said. "I was too young, and ignorant, and probably pretty stupid, trying to hold things together." She stepped back and eyed him with more confidence. "When I learned about Paul's paternity—"

His stance was adversarial, his feet slightly apart, his hands spread across both hips just under his belt. "That's another little detail that's hard to forgive," he broke in. "Your hiding that fact for over twelve years. You were never going to tell anyone, were you?"

She gasped in shock. "I didn't *know*—"

He narrowed his eyes in disbelief. "You had to know Charlotte was pregnant when we were still seeing each other, and you kept it from me. Why? Because it was obvious the baby was Paul's?"

"Believe me, I didn't know *that*," she insisted.

"Just as you didn't *know* your father manipulated witnesses to deny that Charlotte actually stole Paul's car that night? Just as you didn't *know* Charlotte left Paul in the lake to drown when she could have saved him? Just as you didn't *know* she was angry at him for breaking off their engagement?" He glared at her for a few moments, then added, in a lower voice, "Just as you didn't think *I* would know you were carrying on with Rollie Morris while you and I were…comforting each other on weekends."

There was so much to explain, so many lies and manipulations, it would take a lengthy sit-down conversation to describe it all to him. "I didn't betray you. I didn't lie to you," she said firmly, knowing it was inadequate. But the truth would have to wait. "I don't ask for forgiveness, Kale, because you're wrong about my betrayal, but you do know, don't you, that your holding all this anger inside is hurting you the most?"

"I think I've heard this before," he said, his expression droll. "New-age behavioral science, isn't it?"

"Do you think maybe we can put it all behind us for now? And talk to each other without accusing?" She knew better than to expect it, however.

"I'll give it my best effort," he said.

"Will you agree that neither of us should say anything to Amanda until we both agree the time is right?"

He hesitated as if to allow his lingering pain to pass. "Yes, I agree with that."

"Your mother..." she murmured, walking slowly. "She's been hurt so much already."

"It will give her hope, maybe," Kale said.

"Hope?"

"She's had no hope."

They walked in silence through the trees until they came to the parking lot and Kale stopped, sank his hands into his pockets and looked at her, his black eyes unreadable. "What did you expect was going to happen?"

"I don't know."

"Did you ever think about it?"

"About Amanda being Paul's daughter? I've thought of it constantly over the last year. About Paul's death? I had nightmares. It wasn't until I married Rollie that I learned to sleep through the night," she said, and then regretted again revealing so much of herself. "I still think about Paul. And you. I've prayed for you for years, that things would get better." The last came out in a whisper.

"For me? I don't need things to get any better for me. I have everything I've ever wanted, except for my big brother," he said.

"I'm sorry about your parents being unable to recover. My mother and dad live in California. Our relationship has never again been close, not since the accident. They visit, usually, in the summer. Like a duty thing."

He nodded grimly.

"I have no control over what they do or what they say."
She eyed him pointedly. "I never have."

"It was your father who first hinted that you were in a
relationship with the old guy at the Kenross airport," he said.
"Our neighbor Wally Cross confirmed it. Wally told us a lot
of things about your *role* in the Caldwell family."

"I wondered who told you those things. Charlotte didn't
know at the time what was going on either, according to the
letter she left me," she said.

"Charlotte married within two weeks of Paul's death. And
you—apparently the Morris family offered solid resources to
the Caldwell sisters."

It had been her father, she knew now, manipulating them
both for his own ends. She wanted to tell Kale, but not now,
not when the painful truth lay so starkly raw and naked before
them.

He wouldn't believe her anyway, she thought, if she admitted she had only had eyes for him back then, but he had
sent her away. She had felt...discarded. Rollie Morris had
been there when she needed someone.

Kale made a search of her face, as if for an answer, but she
had none to give him.

She had hoped for a miracle, for healing words to come to
her to dispel the bitterness and to ease the tragic effects of the
past.

But they parted in silence.

Five

———

Before leaving the office, Kale Noble had slipped the contents of his in-basket into his briefcase, and now as the plane soared he began the methodical chore of jotting notes to his secretary.

Earphones blotted the roar of the engines and isolated him from casual conversation with the two staff engineers in the back seat. He had discovered after his first air trip to the northern job site that the hour-long flight was a perfect time to dispense with the demands of his in-basket.

He pulled a memo from the case and started to read.

It had been six days since he had last seen Jessi and learned that Amanda was his niece.

He remembered every word and sensation during their conversation, including the thrill of knowing Paul had left behind a child. He also recalled his rage at Jessi not only for betraying him years ago but for continuing to deceive him so that he didn't know what to believe.

She obviously meant to deny Amanda her Noble heritage. But Kale wasn't going to let that happen. He hadn't yet told his parents the news, for he knew they would want to see their granddaughter as soon as possible, and he wasn't sure Amanda was ready for that yet.

She was a gift, hidden from them for more than a decade by Caldwell greed.

He was anxious to tell his mother and to see the rare smile of radiance on her face when he did. He wondered what would happen when they went to the basement where his father now dwelled during his waking hours, maintaining a shrine to his deceased son.

As much as Kale had loved and admired his older brother, he always had an urge to smash the wall of photos, trophies and memorabilia revered by his father.

Down in his father's sanctuary, when it was just the two of them, Kale had mentioned Jessi.

"Caldwell?" his father had questioned. "Charlotte Caldwell killed my son, you know, and got off scot-free. Jessi? She was a good little girl." He had returned to his carving, muttering to himself. "Too good for that family. She was too good for them. If Paul had gone for her instead of the wild one, he'd still be alive."

Then, though he seemed to drift back to his other world, he had continued. "I told him," he'd mumbled. "I told him that Charlotte was no good. And she killed him. She killed him and got away with it."

"Not entirely, Dad," Kale had said gently. "She died last year in a plane crash."

He had seemed not to hear. "Got off scot-free," he'd muttered.

Kale had glanced at the pictures once again, larger-than-life pictures of Paul playing hockey in college, throwing a baseball in middle school, sitting astride his motorcycle in high school, posing with the family at picnics and around the tree at Christmas, standing by the Noble Engineering sign in a business suit.

His sandy blond hair was unmistakable, tight curls and

waves hugging his scalp. He'd had their father's square jaw and intense blue eyes. He had been his father's son, his father's very life.

Kale had no more been able to fill the bleak space Paul left behind than he had been able to get his father's attention when Paul was alive.

He had hope now, though, that bringing Amanda onto the scene might change things.

Tense feelings between the Noble and Caldwell families had sprung up immediately after the accident, especially when it was rumored that Paul had asked Charlotte to return the engagement ring, and Charlotte had grabbed his keys and charged for the sports car. She was stomping on the gas when Paul risked his life to yank a door open and leap inside in an obvious attempt to stop her.

She had sped less than five hundred feet before she crashed through the bridge railing over the lake and plunged to the bottom. Charlotte swam free. Paul, unconscious and bleeding, drowned in the murky water. "I tried to save him!" she had screamed, but there had been no witnesses to that.

Not at first, anyway. Paul was barely in the ground when witnesses "appeared."

Those who had reported that Paul had broken the engagement that night changed their stories. Charlotte had not tried to steal his car, they said now. Nobody could hide the fact, however, that Paul was in the passenger seat at the bottom of the lake. The Caldwells could not manipulate that bit of information.

Charlotte, it was officially decided, was not culpable. However, she had suffered such grievous shock that she ran away and married an old Up North friend she had known since her teenage years.

It all sounded as phony and contrived now as it had then, he mused.

Kale's memory drifted as he gazed absently at the Easter blue sky stretching beyond the plane's window.

If he lived to be a hundred and ten, he would still remember those momentous months following Paul's death when he gradually grew from an awkward, naive boy into a human machine driven by rage, wired by a compulsive tenacity and insulated by the tough scars of a broken heart.

He hadn't thought of it for years, the morning after the accident, when he stood in horror in the kitchen while his mother brokenly reported what he had slept through during that night. No sooner had she made her painful announcement than fifteen-year-old Jessi Caldwell had burst through the back door, a terry-cloth bathrobe barely hiding her nightgown, hair frizzed like an unkempt poodle, little bits of branches and leaves clinging like fuzz from tearing through the hedge that separated their yards.

Mostly he remembered her large tear-filled eyes as she halted abruptly before him, as if he were the only person left in the world. "I just heard...oh, Kale...oh my God...I can't believe... Oh, Kale, it can't be true...tell me it's just a really really bad dream, and I'm not awake yet."

Then she had rushed against him and grasped him hard around the ribs, and he had enfolded her small body. He felt her body racked with sobs, and he watched his own silent tears dripping down the back of her robe, like raindrops tumbling over a towel.

At that moment, when the worst tragedy in his life had just been announced, and he was trying to fathom how he would go on without his brother, he found the sweetest respite he would ever know in the arms of the frizzy-haired tomboy next door.

Her body had felt frail and soft, but her powerful spirit soothed his heart and filled him with something profound and sweet, covering him in a curious softness and offering him a gentle promise of loving solace.

His tender feelings for her were no longer what he imagined he would feel for a kid sister, but the feelings of a potent young man who had found the young woman who owned his heart and soul.

He remembered watching Jessi throw herself on his mother that morning crying, "Oh Reggie Mom, oh Reggie Mom."

Now, thirteen years later, he thought bitterly that she had simply slipped between his good sense and natural caution at a time when he was vulnerable, and she had captured his affections because of the tragic circumstances.

But when he was eighteen, inexperienced with girls, ignored by his father, unsure about the future, and wondering what to do with all those clashing hormones, well, he had simply been too innocent and confused to realize how vulnerable he was to the beguiling teenage girl.

He could see that now. Even though he still remembered the exquisite sensations of holding Jessi Caldwell in his arms.

After that, he and Jessi seemed naturally to refuel each other, revitalize each other's spirits, restore each other's strength, like symbiotic organisms, he thought, dependent upon each other for life-giving energy.

What a foolish boy he had been. Not a man at all. Just a dumb kid learning the bitter consequences of giving his heart to a girl who didn't value it.

He barely remembered now how it had been to feel gloriously in love, waiting for the weekends when Jessi caught a ride with Charlotte's new husband from Up North, or one of the other Morrises who owned the airport by Fancy Acres. If anybody mentioned the name of Kenross, he didn't remember it.

He buried himself in school while what was left of his family was falling apart around him, and he counted the hours until Jessi came back and brought life once again into his days. Sometimes she was back for several weekends in a row, and then sometimes it was several weeks before she came again.

During her Christmas vacation she visited for only a few days, and they carefully avoided mention of the shattered Caldwell-Noble Christmas Eve tradition.

In February when the Caldwell house went up for sale, Jessi explained, "The house is too big now that half the family is gone."

"Does that mean you're never coming back?"

She had eyed him soulfully. "Maybe when Charlotte gets things together. She needs me now. She shouldn't have run away and married Frank so quickly. I don't think she loves him. I think she was in shock over Paul."

"People say Paul broke it off with Charlotte that night," he had told her finally.

"That was a nasty rumor," Jessi had defended her sister. "No such thing happened."

But a few months later, he discovered that the owner of the bar had been an acquaintance of Brad Caldwell, their father, and that witnesses had been warned things would not be as loose and open for favored customers if it were known Charlotte Caldwell had been drinking that night.

And then in the spring, the bar got a face-lift, and all the new furniture came from one of Brad Caldwell's warehouse stores.

Still, Jessi insisted Kale was simply hearing "nasty rumors." She would know, she said, if her parents were involved in anything shady like that.

Meanwhile, Kale's father's personality was already beginning to deteriorate, and he was dragging things out of Paul's room to his basement workshop. They didn't know yet that he would eventually build a macabre shrine to his dead son.

Still, Kale was assuming Jessi was his future. While he was dreaming of marriage and children, however, she was part of the conspiracy to hide Paul's child from the Nobles.

When Brad Caldwell had aroused Kale's suspicions, Jessi's soft assurances had calmed him. She had seemed so innocent.

Kale heard that Brad Caldwell had made a remark to a friend that Charlotte and Frank Morris had been seeing each other for years. They had met when Charlotte was a young girl, when the family was spending a month out of each summer at the Fancy Acres cabin.

He had heard it often enough during the years, the Caldwells' references to the Fancy Acres cabin, which they all loved.

Funny, he thought now, many years later, that he had never been aware the nearest town was Kenross. Nor had he ever bothered to remember the name Morris. It simply hadn't meant anything to him. It never had mattered to him what Charlotte Caldwell's new husband's name was.

It had mattered, though, when he drove sixteen-year-old Jessi to the Crystal Airport one Sunday afternoon to catch her ride with one of Charlotte's in-laws.

He remembered the disturbing sensation when the stocky, good-looking pilot ignored him to smile fondly at Jessi and then guided her possessively into his single-engine plane. Jessi hadn't turned to wave at Kale until they were taxiing away.

At the time, Kale had tamped down the sickening feeling there was something more between them than an in-law relationship. The guy seemed too old for her. She was only sixteen. He had to be in his thirties.

Now he knew it had been Rollie Morris, and three years later Jessi had married him.

Then, late that summer twelve years ago, Wally Cross made it a point to tell him the Caldwells were making fools of the Nobles and everyone but the Nobles knew it. He referred to Jessi as "mature for her age" and headed for marriage with a guy who owned an airport. Had the comment originated from Brad Caldwell, Kale would have been suspicious. But everyone knew Wally Cross was a reliable guy, and no admirer of Brad's.

Still, when Kale finally blew up, when all the pieces of evidence grew into an overwhelming weight that was too heavy to carry anymore, he had hoped she would argue with him, tell him he was wrong.

It was the annual Noble reunion when he confronted her.

Bad timing, he realized later. It was the last one hosted by his parents, a startlingly somber occasion much like Paul's funeral. When everyone was in the backyard, he had pulled Jessi into the living room alcove and exploded with an anger born of long-simmering anguish.

He accused, ignoring her phony astonishment and the silent tears filling her eyes. He had started with the accident, Charlotte's negligence, their father's manipulations, and he let her know he was aware of Jessi's role as emissary and distraction in her family's machinations. Her sweet innocence had been the perfect front, the perfect lull, in the Caldwell cover-up. And then he told her he knew about the pilot she had been carrying on with Up North while on weekends she pretended she was in love with him.

Then he stopped and waited for her to refute all he had said, so the nightmare would end. He certainly hadn't wanted to lose her. He had loved her.

But she merely covered her face with her hands, and when he turned around, he saw that all his relatives had come into the house and were in the living room, grim and earnest witnesses to his angry accusations.

When he turned back to Jessi, he softened for a moment, but she turned her back and strode away.

Sympathy was definitely with him, he observed as he watched her leave.

No one spoke until several moments after she had gone, and then they praised him for opening his eyes and seeing what they had apparently seen long ago.

So he learned that she had not defended herself because she had had no defense.

It was a bitter lesson for a nineteen-year-old.

It was the third week in July, only six days since Jessi's last upsetting meeting with Kale, and he was coming back today. It was nine in the morning, and his plane would be arriving any minute.

Burness Contracting was pouring forms on the Kenross end of the bridge today. Hundreds of yards of forms were to be poured during the next week, and Kale Noble wanted to over-see the beginning of it. Curt Burness had told Chaz about it, and Kale's secretary had called to reserve the rental car for the day.

He was bringing two engineers with him, Kale's secretary had told Chaz, who had established a friendly long-distance relationship with her.

That he was bringing two of his company staff was good news to Jessi, for she knew after their last encounter that she should never again allow herself to be alone with him.

Shortly before his plane arrived, there was an emergency call for air ambulance, and Chaz left in a hurry. When Kale arrived, she was behind the desk to hand him the rental key and meet the attractive, well-dressed couple with him.

"Mike Carlson, my assistant, and Londa Jergens, one of the engineers who worked on the design of the Point Six," Kale said before he reached for the keys.

Londa was a tall blonde, slender and attractive. With a little effort in the makeup and hair departments she would be glam-orous. Jessi wondered, had she been to Grand Cayman? Then she caught herself. It was none of her business.

"You drive," Kale said as he pulled the door open and tossed the keys to Mike.

"Nice to meet you, Jessi," Mike said with a quick wave and preceded Kale out the door. Londa followed without a word, as if Jessi weren't in the room.

Jessi turned her head away, looking down at the glass counter and the little brass wings attached to a pair of earrings for sale. She heard the door close, and they were gone.

Was that the kind of woman Kale wanted? Smart, well-educated and professional to boot. An engineer. A beautiful blonde who designed bridges. Perfect match, wasn't it? Noble Engineering would be a nice family business again, ripe and ready for another generation.

Another generation. Kale should have children of his own and be content to let Amanda live with her.

Why did it hurt? It was no business of hers. He meant nothing to her but a threat, if he tried to take Amanda away. She hadn't thought of him for years, until he flew into her life again. She certainly didn't need him in her life.

Let the beautiful blonde have him, all of him, with his attitude and all that bitterness.

She didn't want to remember that he had apologized to her, that she had heard remorse in his voice, and seen anguish in his face, that for a moment by the lake there had been just a hint of the old vulnerability in his manner. She didn't want to remember the exhilaration when his hard body pressed against her or the tenderness when he kissed her. She didn't want to be reminded that it was pain, much of it caused by her own adolescent mistakes, that underlay his bitter anger.

Chaz was back at noon after having taken a heart attack victim from a neighboring town to the Virginia Hospital eighty miles northeast of Kenross. About three, Amanda burst in for her afternoon hug, and then told Jessi that her computer teacher had taken the class to watch the big event at the Point Six bridge site.

"They're pouring concrete for the bridge supports into these humongous frames that go right down into the swamp, and there are plastic-coated steel reinforcing bars so that the ice can't break them in winter. And there are flat barges to haul the wet cement, and long tubes—my teacher said it's a historic occasion because it's the first time this kind of bridge has been built over a swamp, and computers were used in the design. Three-dimensional computers! And I saw Mr. Noble there telling people what to do, and looking at some big rolled-up papers. My teacher said they were blueprints."

Jessi smiled and ruffled Amanda's short curly hair.

Amanda erupted with more. "And do you know why they call it the Point Six? It's exactly six tenths of a mile long. We've been calling it that so long I never stopped to think why," Amanda rushed on. "I felt so important. I called to Mr. Noble and waved, and he smiled and he said 'hi, Amanda' and all the kids were impressed. It was neat, Jessi. Did he really design the Point Six?"

"I believe so. His company did, at any rate. He owns Noble Engineering," she said.

Amanda spent the rest of the afternoon fueling airplanes, running errands and talking to people coming and going around the place. When there was a lull, she watched Pelly work on an engine. Jessi saw the girl's eyes dart periodically toward the rental car parking place, knowing she was watching for Kale's return.

When he did, it was not a joyous reunion, however, for Kale was striding and glaring, his arms full of several large rolls of paper, obviously plans. Londa and Mike were scurrying behind him. Phil the pilot appeared, and the four of them had a hurried conference before Kale stormed into the office and dropped his rolls onto the counter where they bounced in different directions and Amanda scooped them together in an orderly pile.

Jessi watched him from the doorway, frowning, seeing that something was wrong, not wanting to ask.

"I need a place to stay tonight, maybe for a few days," he said. "How's that motel by the industrial park?"

"Full," Jessi said. "Tourists and construction workers."

"Anywhere else around here? A hotel? Anything."

"We can call around," she said.

Londa came in. "Let me stay with you," she pleaded softly, standing behind Kale. "I can help. I'm familiar with this part of the design."

"No," he said. "It looks as though there's a shortage of rooms."

"We can share—"

"No, I want you to go back with Mike," he said quietly.

Her eyes flared for a moment, and her lips pouted. "I'm

not asking for the moon, dammit,'' she spat, her voice very low.

He swung around impatiently, but gentled his voice before he replied, ''I think Phil is holding the plane for you.'' He turned swiftly to Jessi. ''Can you get me a telephone book?''

''I can call for you,'' Amanda offered, her face eager, eyes wide, as she reached into a drawer in the cabinet behind the counter and pulled out a regional telephone book.

Jessi watched Londa walking stiffly to the Noble plane where Mike and the pilot were already waiting. Then Mike called to Londa, holding out a small athletic bag. She merely batted at it when she got within reach, and Mike jumped out and trotted to the office with the bag.

''You might need this,'' he said, handing it to Kale. Then he raced back to the plane which prepared to leave.

''You may not find a place,'' Jessi warned Kale as he and Amanda looked through the yellow pages and Amanda dialed both of the other motels in town.

Jessi wandered to the lounge and watched the aircraft take off without its owner. Kale was going to have some fences to mend when he returned home, she thought. Then she heard Amanda's excited voice.

''Hey, I have a great idea. Why don't you stay with us? We have an extra bedroom, and you can use the dining room table to spread out your drawings. It's better than a motel room any day. If we could even find one.''

As Jessi turned to protest, she met Kale's eyes, for he, too, had turned at the same time, apparently also to protest, and they read in each other's eyes, the deep desire they both wished to deny and the great fear of its consequences. What she read in his eyes in that moment was probably similar to what she felt within herself, the quandary of facing the exquisite thrill of failing to emerge unscathed from what could lie ahead.

It was a silent communion they shared because it was not something either of them could—or would—put into words.

"It's settled!" Amanda declared, slapping closed the telephone book and grinning at her speechless aunt at the other end of the lounge.

Six

Jessi tried to see her small cottage through Kale's eyes. It would surely be rough and tiny by his standards.

The guest room was small and square. It had been a guest room for as long as Jessi had lived in the house, from the time of her wedding nine and a half years before.

Amanda's room had always been hers, for even when she had lived with her parents on the other side of town, she had frequently stayed a night or a weekend with Jessi, sometimes longer when Charlotte was, well, suffering and out of sorts.

Amanda was the one who led Kale to the cottage, dancing attendance on the tall, dark man with the briefcase and the armload of drawings. Amanda had the athletic bag slung proudly over one shoulder and her school bag over the other. Jessi watched them cross the parking lot to the path through the woods leading to the cottage.

She watched Amanda's enthusiasm and hoped it would be an adequate buffer between her and Kale for the day or two that he would be staying. She had given instructions to

Amanda to sprinkle a chicken with herbs and put it in the oven and to make a salad. Jessi explained awkwardly to Kale that she would have dual students until about eight-thirty.

"You and Amanda eat without me," she had said, avoiding his eyes. "She can show you where everything is. I'll be home late."

When she had finally let her eyes drift up to his face, she found him studying her, his dark eyes burning into her, forcing her to look away again after only a few seconds. *I think I'll be very, very late getting home tonight,* she decided.

Her stomach flopped at the thought of Kale invading her home, undressing, crawling between the sheets, sleeping the night and awakening in the morning, sharing the bathroom. One bathroom had always seemed adequate.

Ordinarily she'd have gone home to eat before meeting with her students, but tonight, she made herself busy. After all, Amanda had been delighted that she could play grown-up with this important man who had called her by name in front of her computer class.

When they disappeared from sight, Jessi thought about Amanda and the Nobles, and how they probably had as much right to her guardianship as she did. And then she thought back through the years.

Memories flooded out the present, burying her in regrets she had hoped never to re-live. There were all those *if onlys* that had never happened.

If only her parents had confided their fears and intentions.

If only she had looked more closely at their faces, listened more closely to their words, questioned them face-to-face about their motivations during that time.

If only she had been forthright and open with Kale, expressed her fears and vague suspicions, instead of trying to maintain a harmony she hoped would spread to both of their families so that things could be the way they had been before the accident.

If only she had concentrated more on being honest than on sparing Kale's feelings.

If only, in the end, she had spoken up in her own defense and refused to be stymied by the astonishment and hurt that grew into anger.

If only she had stopped to think of the future and how much Kale really meant to her.

But her parents had lied to her, and she had not pursued the niggling suspicions that they were conspiring but had taken them at their word that initial rumors were wrong, that Charlotte had tried to save Paul in the lake, that they had not interfered in the natural evolution of events, that they had not deliberately fabricated rumors that would affect what Kale believed about her.

They had lied.

Again and again they had lied, manipulating events to protect Charlotte and themselves.

It had all been revealed to Jessi, finally, in the letter Charlotte left behind, a letter she had written ten years before and given to Frank's attorney in Kenross. She had written the letter, she said, to ease her conscience, but Jessi suspected it had not done that, for Charlotte had remained a lost soul, relentlessly haunted, alternately reckless and depressed. She had never stopped mourning, or feeling guilty.

Their parents had known Charlotte was pregnant with Paul's baby, and had encouraged her to flee north to elope with Frank, who had always been crazy about her. Charlotte's letter revealed that, too.

Kale had every right to despise the lot of them, for they had deceived and manipulated, and Jessi had been an important pawn in carrying out the lies, although she had been too naive at the time to recognize that.

She had been in love. As if a fifteen-year-old girl wasn't foolish enough just being fifteen and ignorant, but she had been fifteen and so smitten by the boy next door she could think of little else.

The whole world had seemed shaded with gentleness, and time had been skewed to plod more slowly when she was away from Kale and to sprint when they were together. She remembered how perceptive he was of her moods, how thoughtful of her feelings, how sensitive to her. She was beautiful and graceful when she was with him because he saw her that way. He was strong and honest, tall and rugged.

She had loved the way he looked. The other girls thought he was too coarse in the face, but she loved the crevasses and lines, and the hard edge to his cheekbones. She loved how tall he was. She loved to watch him play basketball, admiring his body and the way he moved.

Mostly, she had loved the strength of his integrity, which she had not recognized or put a name to until she was old enough to realize its value.

She should have protested immediately when he accused her of betrayal. But her astonishment was paralyzing, and the hurt left her fighting tears. When she saw the hostile audience of people she had thought were friends, she felt an anger so deep and overwhelming, she could think only of maintaining her pride while she got away as quickly as possible.

Jessi had felt as if *she* were the one betrayed, as if she had been set up by Kale's family because he didn't want her hanging around anymore, a stupid, lovesick little teenager taking up nearly all his weekends. She wouldn't give them the satisfaction of seeing her beg to be heard.

She had been overwhelmed with a need to bury herself somewhere deep and quiet. When her temper cooled, she realized she might have been mistaken about Kale's sinister intent. He might simply have been misled by gossip.

But by the time she had run back to Kenross, *later* became *never*.

The Caldwells sold the house in Minneapolis and moved to California, where they started a new life without their daughters.

Of course, they visited every summer, for they would not

give up the month's vacation at Fancy Acres. But it was never the same. Jessi never set foot on Fancy Acres after her sixteenth birthday. She no longer had anything in common with her mousy mother and dour father.

She missed them, the parents she had known as a child, but she rejected who they had become.

College held little appeal, for she saw a cozy secure future with the Morrises, and she felt alone and isolated for her short time on the lovely St. Cloud State University campus. Then, too, Charlotte ran away during the middle of Jessi's third quarter, and she had to return home to take care of Amanda.

By the time Charlotte wandered back home, penitent and distraught, it was too late for Jessi to recapture her studies, and she simply dropped out.

She married Rollie after his second proposal, and it had been a good life for Jessi until the plane crash took away most of her family.

Even so, she and Amanda were recovering nicely.

Until Kale Noble dropped like a surprise attack on their lovely little world.

When the last of her flight school students was gone, she gassed the plane and secured it in the hangar, then she swept the hangar and took the vacuum to the interior of the trainer. Even that didn't seem to eat up enough time.

When it was nearing eleven, she locked up and walked home. As she stepped onto the open front porch facing the lake, she hesitated, knowing it was Kale sitting on the porch swing in the dark, even though she couldn't see him.

"I thought you'd be asleep," she said, her voice hushed.

"I thought so, too," he replied softly.

"If your room is too warm, there's a fan in the back porch," she said, grasping the handle of the screen door.

"It isn't," he replied, a low, disembodied voice from the end of the porch.

"Do you need anything?" she asked, hesitant and trembling, gripping the handle hard.

"Yes," he said.

She sensed him moving toward her, although she couldn't see him, and when she felt his body heat, she saw his faint outline in the residual light from the living room.

"Peace," he said. "I need some peace."

Charges, fast and quick, prickled her skin, and she inhaled deeply and dropped her chin to fight them. If she looked up, he might kiss her and, heaven help her, she might enjoy it very much.

"It's very peaceful here," she said, knowing what she spoke of had little to do with the kind of peace he referred to.

"So it would appear," he whispered. "So peaceful you stayed away until you thought I was safely tucked away in bed?"

She felt his hand on her arm, below her shoulder, grasping lightly. It was the gentleness of his grasp that made her want to lean against him. She thought with desperation of what to say.

"Why did you have to stay? What happened?" she asked, steeling herself against his touch.

His hand dropped away. He hesitated a moment, and then said, "A design flaw. I saw it right away when the pouring got underway. I think I can correct it."

"Will you have to stop the pouring?"

"No. It isn't in the supports."

"Then how did you see it? The flaw, I mean."

"I saw the bridge completed, in my mind, and it just... happened. I saw the flaw. I saw the supports and...it was like an illumination, very obvious, something I should have seen before." His voice was low, hushed, as though he were confiding something from deep in his consciousness.

"What would happen if you didn't correct it? If you hadn't seen it?" she asked.

"The bridge would be imperfect," he replied.

"Unsafe?"

"No. Less than it can be," he said.

"Is it necessary that it be perfect?"

"If possible," he replied. "But there will be other flaws. There always are. We just don't catch them, sometimes not for years."

"Because you're not perfect," she said.

"No, I'm not perfect." She heard his soft sigh, wondering if it was regret or acceptance, or something else. She couldn't see his face and didn't know what he was thinking.

The silence that followed was dangerous, so she broke it, asking, "How long will it take you?"

"I don't know. Longer than a day or two, I think," he said.

"Is it so hard for you, having me here?"

She hesitated, pulled the screen door open and stepped inside. "Yes," she confessed in a whisper. He followed her through the screen door. She went to the kitchen sink and poured a glass of water.

"Is this where you lived with Rollie? Was this his house?"

"Yes, we lived here. We bought it before the wedding. I painted all the rooms before we moved in, and we picked out the furniture together," she told him, letting her eyes roam over the open living room and kitchen toward the alcove where there was a small dining room with a wall of small square-paned windows overlooking what had been her shade flower garden before Rollie died. "I was nineteen and I had dropped out of college. Charlotte needed help with Amanda, and Frank, uh, was still learning...to cope." Her voice faded to a whisper.

It appalled her that those words slipped out because she didn't like to admit, even to herself, that it had been so easy to marry Rollie to provide an alternate home for Amanda. But she had grown to love Rollie. She had. Everybody loved Rollie. You just couldn't help but love a man like that.

"To cope? With Charlotte?" Kale finished her sentence.

There seemed little point in denying it. There had been too

many lies in the way of their relationship a dozen years ago, and anyway, Kale had known Charlotte and her impulsive behavior before Paul's accident. "Yes," she replied. "You remember how she was. She never changed," she admitted woefully. Everyone had known Charlotte was a little reckless, dashing into things without stopping to think of consequences.

He was silent for a moment. He probably knew more about Charlotte's young escapades than she did. But he had apparently decided to be diplomatic, and changed the subject. "I'm sorry my being here annoys you, but I'm getting to know Amanda, and that's worth something."

It was worth a gigantic bushel of fear for Jessi.

She batted down her trepidation. "Make yourself at home tomorrow. Help yourself to whatever you need. Spread out your plans wherever you—"

"I already have," he interrupted. "You haven't seen your dining room table."

"It's all right," she said. "I won't be here much."

He nodded curtly, swallowing his obvious discomfort. "Good night, then."

As he moved toward the hallway to the bedrooms, she called to him softly. "And Kale?" He stopped as though for a prison guard, not turning to face her, his profile grim. "Tomorrow night, maybe it would be a good idea if you were asleep when I come home." It was an order, however softly spoken. He couldn't miss it, she knew.

He remained still. "Why?" She saw the tight pull of his cheeks and knew he was swallowing more than a little anger. He was furious. And he was at her mercy, in her home, dependent upon her largesse, which was minimal, and given with obvious and great reluctance.

"I don't think I need to give you an explanation," she whispered.

He turned slowly toward her, shadows from the single light emphasizing the rugged carving of his features. "As I recall, you never were much for explanations," he said softly, and then he moved slowly toward her until he was looking down at her upturned face. "But I can draw my own conclusions," he whispered. "You're as affected as I am, and as curious."

"Curious?"

"About this," he murmured, and tipped her chin so that he could lower his face and touch his lips to hers, not in the sweet gentle kiss of their youth, but in a demanding, erotic gesture that spoke of worldliness and experience.

The kiss took her breath away, and she gasped when he pulled apart to study her eyes in the shadowy light. But he returned, slipping his hard arms around her and deepening the pressure of his mouth, invading and penetrating, stirring a wild passion she had never known with her late husband.

She grasped him around the ribs and pinched his shirt between her fingers, off balance, lost, consumed, burning.

She couldn't have put into words what she had dreaded from him, but now she knew.

It had been her own reaction. And with good reason.

The kiss went on forever, but ended too soon. Another threatening indication that she was out of her mind. She wanted him gone far away, and she wanted him to kiss her again. One was her brain speaking, the other her heart.

Obviously, her will to resist him was much too fragile. She recognized that as she watched him stroll casually to the guest room, hesitate, and then disappear for the night behind the closed door.

Jessi stood alone in the room, hugging herself in a vain attempt to breathe normally and to stop the trembling that shook her. She reached for the cabinet and leaned against it, her eyes pressed closed. Damn him, she thought. Damn Kale Noble for his power over her.

Jessi took over Chaz's jobs the next night, and flew the helicopter on an ambulance run when it was actually his turn to be on call. She extended her day to its limit, and dropped exhausted into a chair at ten-thirty.

Suddenly the screen door opened and Kale burst into the room, his face the image of thunder. "What in the hell are you doing here?" he demanded.

She was stunned and too weary to respond.

"I'm taking you home," he said. He moved swiftly, taking her hand, pulling her to the door.

"You can let go of my hand."

He did. "There's no need for this, Jessi," he said, walking by her side. "I'll pitch a tent before I'll drive you from your home another night."

"Go ahead," she muttered. "There's one stored in the gazebo."

He seemed not to hear her. "Amanda was upset tonight. I took it upon myself to let her go on an overnight with her friend down the road. She suspects you don't like me, and she's feeling very guilty that she invited me."

"Poor Kale," she teased.

"Dammit, Jessi, I'm sorry to impose on you like this, but it's done, and neither of us can do much about it at this point without hurting Amanda's feelings," he said with vehemence. "Now I think I can wind up things in another day or so. Would it be asking the impossible for you to adhere to your usual schedule?"

"I suppose I can manage for another day," she said.

"You're beat."

"I had an ambulance run," she said. "The patient may not make it, and he was one of Rollie's friends."

He paused for a few seconds, and then put an arm around her shoulder as they walked. "I'm sorry, Jessi," he said softly.

She shrugged away from him. "Don't touch me," she said, shaken, near tears. "I don't want you ever to touch me again."

"All right," he replied, his voice still soft. "I won't touch you again."

"And don't be nice. Or talk to me in that tone of voice. I don't want you to be nice to me, do you hear?" Her voice cracked and she almost laughed at her own desperation, but she was limp with fatigue and irrational with fear that he would kiss her and hold her again and she would lose it. Again.

"Impossible," he replied. "I'm never nice."

"I'm just tired," she muttered.

"I know. Want to have a swim before bed?"

"A swim?" she sputtered, stopping in her tracks. "A swim! With you? In my lake?"

He put a hand over her mouth and grinned. His face was red in the reflection of the neon lights from the restaurant. "No need to invite everybody," he cautioned, gesturing toward the restaurant's bar where the door was propped open.

She slapped his hand away. "I'd feel safer with sixteen piranha," she retorted, storming away toward her cottage.

"Why would you feel safer?" he taunted, catching up with her effortlessly, his long legs adjusting to her pace.

"They just...bite," she said, her voice disappearing with the last word. No, they don't touch me so that sensations shoot everywhere. They aren't tender and seductive. They might bite and be painful, but I'd know enough to fight them.

"And I don't?" He was incredulous.

"I'm not afraid of your sharp teeth," she said.

"Then what is it that scares you, Jessi?" he asked, and she took a deep breath to replace what seemed to be leaking from her lungs, for it was patently obvious that he knew exactly what he was doing to her and what she was afraid of.

"Just don't touch me, Kale Noble," she warned. "You just stay away from me."

"I'm not touching you," he said, lifting his hands in the air.

She eyed him, wondering where this teasing, good-humored version of him had come from, wondering if it was contrived to sweet-talk her into accepting his presence in her home, wondering if it was a seduction, wondering if, perhaps, it was madness of a sort. His madness, of course, not hers.

As they neared the cabin, she veered off. "I think I will

have a swim, but you stay away, do you hear? I want to swim alone.''

She strode toward the dock, unbuttoning her shirt and pulling it out of her short split skirt. At the end of the dock she dropped the blouse and her bra and pushed her skirt and underwear over her hips and let them drop. She removed her shoes and dove into the familiar water.

Why water in the darkness of night felt intimately silky against her skin had always baffled her. The same water in the light of day was cold and smooth, but never silky, never caressing and warm like water in the night. She swam straight out from the dock toward a single yellow light across the lake, a familiar guiding light.

And then she ducked under the water, feeling energized and playful. When she broke the surface, she looked for the yellow dot across the lake and the lights from her cottage windows to line herself up where she knew it was comfortable to swim in the utter blackness.

Finally, she felt a chill and the languid tremor that told her it was time to return to land. As she neared the dock, she was aware of another swimmer nearby, and she stopped to tread water. ''Kale?''

''Were you expecting someone else?''

''Of course not. I always swim alone at night.''

''It isn't safe,'' he said.

''It's perfectly safe. But if you back up a little, you'll be in the weeds.''

''I know. I already tangled with them.''

''Get back to shore or I'll have to rescue you,'' she warned.

''I'll follow you.''

''No!''

''I won't touch you,'' he said.

''Good. I don't have a suit.''

''Neither do I,'' he replied.

He was coming closer. ''Stay away,'' she hissed.

''I'm away,'' he replied.

She swam then, for all she was worth, back to the dock, a low barely discernible silhouette against the light in the cottage's window. She pulled herself up in the darkness before he got close.

"There are towels on the dock," he called, closer behind her than she had thought. She nearly tripped over her clothes, then squatted to find the towels. When she did, she wrapped one around her torso, and then felt her way to the end of the dock, stepping lightly over the clothes she had shed earlier. She held out the other towel for him.

He pulled himself up on the end of the dock, twisted his back to her and sat. She could see part of his frame against the lights across the lake, the vague outline of muscled triceps, the side of his chest and how he narrowed from his waist down.

She wanted to reach out and run her hand down his back, or his front, over his skin. She handed him the towel, which he used to dry his hair and face and wipe his shoulders.

She stared at his naked silhouette, so close.

Then he rose in one lithe movement and faced her, wrapping the towel around his hips. She could only sense where he was and see part of his shadow. She stooped to scoop up her clothes and led the way to the cottage.

On the porch, before she reached the door, she stopped suddenly, surprised at her own action, reluctant to walk into the lamp light of the cottage where they would stand and face each other in nothing but towels damp from their wet bodies.

What she didn't think about was that he would run into the back of her, and she would feel his cool chest and the hair that grew there pressed momentarily against her upper back where her towel didn't cover. Or that he would fling his arm out around her waist to catch his balance. Or that she would panic at the heat that shot through her, drop the clothes and turn around to push him away, only to find herself cradled against his chest.

Before his hand could drop away from the small of her

back, her arms slid around his neck, and he was kissing her. Hard. Deep. Pulling her against him. Her towel slipped from where she had tucked it under her arm, and only their bodies pressed together and his hand on her lower back held it between them.

He was pushing her backwards until she was up against the table by the porch swing, and then he lifted his hand and pulled away slightly so that the towel fell. He made a slight movement with his arm, and his own towel hit the floor silently.

Then she was back in his arms, sitting against the table and he was working his way between her thighs, gently, erotically, his tongue swirling in her mouth, his warm hands tenderly caressing her cool skin, moving everywhere, shoulders to buttocks, around her ribs, stopping to touch her breasts as though they were precious lace.

She was melting through his skin into his body, forming around him, welcoming the smooth hardness that nudged between her legs, teasing, moving against her and then with her, penetrating through her wetness, slowly, edging inside, very slowly, her body caught in the caress, melting, molding, joining with his, lost in the rapture he wove around her, hungry for him to stretch her wide, to push himself deep inside.

Jessi was vaguely aware that she was raising first one knee and then the other to grip his waist, urging him to slide deeper, pushing herself against him to take more of him. But he held back. He held himself at the entrance to her body, probing in slow small penetrations.

His tongue moved to her lips, and then his lips left hers. "I said I wouldn't touch you, Jessi. I said I wouldn't. Push me away. Tell me to stop."

She instinctively lifted her knees, then squeezed them together across his chest and pushed lightly against him. "Kale," she moaned, feeling him drop away from her, regretting instantly her defensive response to his plea, wanting to capture him again, bring him back, beg him to satisfy the wild ravenous hunger.

He stepped back swiftly, reached down and grabbed up a towel and pulled it around him. He turned away from her. "I'm sorry, Jessi," he groaned, and disappeared down the steps toward the lake. She heard the splash as he hit the cool water.

She perched on the edge of the table and hugged her knees to her chest, breathing in ragged gasps, wondering if the throbbing would ever subside. She could feel him pressing in, hard and smooth, oh so wonderful.

She lowered her feet to the floor of the porch finally, knowing that she was profoundly changed, knowing that she had finally tasted the passion that had all her life, until now, eluded her.

Seven

Jessi arose in the morning, exhausted, confused, dreading her next confrontation with her houseguest. She was astonished to find him at her dining room table immersed in his plans, sketching lines, figuring calculations on a calculator with myriad buttons, while pressing his cell phone to his ear with a hunched shoulder.

He wore a white shirt and shorts, his feet and legs bare, his black straight hair reaching in thick strands over his forehead, a dark stubble on his chin and cheeks giving him an endearing unkemptness that made it difficult for Jessi to watch him without touching.

Amanda burst into the kitchen, dropped her overnight bag on the floor and hurriedly made toast. "I forgot my assignment," she whined, sitting at the table paging through a book while she waited for the toast. "I have to have this read before class," she moaned.

"So stop complaining and read," Jessi advised, smiling, as

she strode through the kitchen and poured herself a cup of coffee.

"You're late this morning," Amanda observed.

"I was late last night, too," Jessi replied, sipping the coffee.

Studying the page before her, Amanda said with anxiety, "I promised Chaz I'd take care of the gas pumps so he could take a charter this morning. And I have to have this read for my computer class."

She heard Kale on the telephone around the corner. His voice was urgent, excited. "Put it on the CAD. Run it through again. I'm sure it will work. It just struck me last night. It solves the balance problem. Yes. Yes. I knew it. Give it to drafting and fax it to Burness as soon as it's done. Thanks, Mike. I'll go over it with Burness as soon as it gets there. I should be home tonight. No, I'll call when I'm sure. Don't send Phil until I call."

"Did he work all night?" Amanda muttered.

"Time to go," Jessi reminded.

"I'm not ready," she wailed. "I just know it will be busy and I won't get any time to study before my class this afternoon."

"You'll find lots of time, Amanda," she assured, a soft hand on her niece's shoulder. "It looks a little cloudy. We might have weather."

Amanda knew what that meant. Bad weather. Weather that prohibited or, at best, limited flying.

"Not likely," she griped and slammed the book shut.

Amanda said goodbye to Kale, kissed Jessi and flew from the house. Jessi sank onto a kitchen chair. Kale came to the table, pulled out a chair opposite her and dropped down. There were gray saucers under his black eyes which burned with bright liquid fire this morning. He looked wonderful, dark, sexy. She closed her eyes against the heat that was building below her belly.

"It came to me early this morning when I was lying awake thinking about you, and trying not to, and wondering what I was going to do about my problem with the bridge. It came to me like poetic inspiration, if I believed in such things.'' His voice was low. ''I dreamed of a shape, and a whole new concept in balance took form. I calculated it and tried to draw it, and this morning Mike put it on the computer, and it's the answer.''

The excitement in his voice was contagious even though it was subdued by his natural restraint, and she almost forgot how awkward she had expected this meeting with him to be. Almost.

''Congratulations,'' she said, warily.

He reached across the table and covered her hand. ''Something inspired me.''

She couldn't decide whether he was being sarcastic or taking a stab at humor. Whatever his intent, the words struck deep, and she instinctively masked their impact by making a droll, disbelieving face at him and pulling her hand away.

''Jessi,'' he started, narrowing his eyes. ''I'm sorry about last night. I'm sorry.... You do that to me, the craziest things, twisting my insides...''

''Stop!'' she cried, holding up a hand. ''Don't apologize,'' she ordered, her voice barely above a whisper. ''I don't even think it was your fault.'' She pushed her chair back and stood abruptly, then flew from the room. He caught her in the doorway to the hall.

''Jessi, I'd be lying if I said I won't touch you again,'' he said, holding her with a hand on her neck and a hand around the back of her waist. ''I want you too much. It isn't sane, wanting you so much.'' He drew in a ragged breath. His eyes burned into her. ''When I come back, it won't be for the bridge,'' he whispered. ''It will be to finish what we've started.''

She stared at him, blinked and opened her mouth to speak but could not think of a thing to utter. She was stunned. Her heart felt as if it were bouncing around in her chest. What was he saying? That he was coming back simply to have sex with her? He was going to satisfy his lust for her, and he expected her cooperation? Was that what he was saying?

Or was he saying he was attracted to her, that he wanted her because he cared for her, had forgiven her and no longer despised her, and remembered how it was to love her.

What was he saying? How could she know?

If she asked, what would she say if he reaffirmed he only wanted her body? What would she say if he told her he was falling in love with her? He wasn't, of course. Just a few short days ago he was as angry with her as he had ever been, and he had been frank about her not being the kind of woman he wanted in his future.

Was it true, as he claimed, that even as a teen, he hadn't truly loved her but only lusted? Then why, so many years ago, had he been so gentle and considerate, never touching her in any way suggestive?

Was this a game he played? Was this part of his vengeance on the Caldwell sisters?

And what of Amanda? Did his parents know yet that Amanda was their granddaughter? Was he taking action to get her away from Jessi?

There were too many questions, bewildering and confounding her so that she couldn't focus on anything but her inability to respond to his words, whatever they meant in terms of his motives.

She felt his hand move up her neck and then she felt her chin caught in the spread of his thumb and index finger. He forced her face up so that she would look at him, but she closed her eyes.

His lips brushed against hers with maddeningly erotic dawdling that turned her muscles and bones to syrup. "Don't be afraid, Jessi," he whispered into her mouth, and she knew in that instant she was no match for his well-honed skills of seduction. She had no defense even when she knew his tender attack was deliberate and practiced.

Gently, slowly, he used his lips and his mouth. He positioned her with artist's hands, and she found herself powerless to be other than his willing subject, mesmerized and pliable in his arms. The experience was too sweet and enthralling to escape and too emotionally lethal to be joyous.

It was the clumping of youthful sneakers across the front porch that separated them finally, abruptly.

Before Amanda burst in, Jessi found herself lightly guided into the kitchen area. As she stood by the doorway, she saw with peripheral vision that Kale had gone the other way and was coming into sight from the dining room.

"Hey, Jessi, you were right. We got weather!" Amanda declared, grinning, letting the screen door slam behind her. The girl turned to Kale. "And you can't leave," she told him in a voice that said she had just defeated him and was the victor in some vague nameless game he didn't know they were playing.

Jessi's eyes riveted on Kale who stood with his weight on one leg and his arms crossed over his chest, grinning at Amanda as though he knew the game well and had somehow scored a winning point in spite of her victory claim. "Is that so?" he challenged.

"We've got weather!" she declared again. "A humongous front!"

"Thunderheads?" Jessi asked.

"Lots," she replied, focusing on her aunt. "A storm front coming from the Dakotas moving toward the Great Lakes. Moving slow. No flying for at least twenty-four hours, Chaz says. The charter's canceled. I'm going to stay here and study for my computer class."

Jessi moved to the screen door, pushed it open and held it so that it closed slowly without slamming. She stepped to the side facing the lake and looked to the west. Even if she hadn't seen the roiling clouds like charcoal cotton, she could feel the impending low pressure, for it was eerily still and dark. In the southern part of the state she would have predicted tornadoes, but they rarely struck so far north, although she recognized they were in for a whale of a beating. Maybe hail. Certainly battering winds and hard rain.

She looked at her float plane in the U-shaped dock and called, "Help me secure the plane!" Amanda knew the procedure well. High winds could destroy a small plane if it wasn't protected.

Kale and Amanda both helped her, and then she and Amanda went to the base while Kale gathered what he needed to visit the bridge site.

Chaz and Jessi made the rounds of the hangars, ensuring that all the doors were securely closed, and then they tied down the wings of the planes that were lined up in rented space on the far side of the field. Most owners didn't bother to secure the wings. Some didn't even bother to place chocks against the wheels when they parked. She and Chaz prepared them for the storm, cursing the negligence of owners who had learned from experience that Jessi was too conscientious to let anyone's plane be destroyed simply because the owner didn't secure it properly.

They removed and stored the chocks that lay alongside the parking apron by the office building, took down the flags, brought in the hanging flower pots and tied down or removed anything that might be damaged or blown away by the approaching storm.

Jessi retreated to her upstairs office to concentrate on endless paperwork. She saw Kale walking across the parking lot, rolls of blueprints tucked under his arm. He was coming for the key. She expected him to reach into the drawer for it, record the mileage and leave in it.

But she heard him coming up the stairs and she braced herself, wishing her heart would not race so that it threatened to burst out of her chest.

She turned to look at him as he stopped on the top step, the blueprints apparently left on the counter downstairs. She watched him survey her space, encircled by glass. He approached her chair and looked over her desk to the south and then the west where the ominous sky was a puffy ceiling of giant blackened pillows swimming aggressively toward them. "Do you expect damage?" he asked.

"Some. Wind is unpredictable," she replied. "There's no way to guarantee that a plane out in the open won't be damaged."

He looked down at her, his black eyes bright and unrelenting with desire.

He might have moved closer, but the telephone rang, and she answered it swiftly. "Kenross Aviation."

"I'm trying to reach Mr. Kale Noble," said a feminine voice.

"He's here. Just a moment." She handed the telephone to him.

"Yes?" he said, then his voice softened. "Yes, Londa. Good morning. I was about to leave for the site. You were lucky to catch me. What is it?" He paused, obviously listening. He began pacing, but was restricted by the cord. He lifted the telephone from her desk and carried it with him so that he could pace.

Jessi stood to leave and allow him privacy, but before she could make it to the stairs, she heard him say, "If you keep this up, you're going to persuade me it was a bad idea to hire you. Yes, you're a helluva engineer. Remember that. Everything else is history. Remember that, too, okay?"

He paced away, facing the airfield. She didn't want to listen. It was none of her business. His voice was restrained and low, as though he were speaking privately to a recalcitrant child.

He turned toward her again and she looked sideways at him as she took the first step down the stairs. She studied his face where a rare frown of compassion created a new crevasse in the middle of his forehead. "I'm leaving for the site shortly. I'll see you in the office tomorrow."

Jessi stopped when she heard the receiver click against the cradle, and she returned slowly to her desk.

When he replaced the receiver, his hand lingered and his

troubled eyes focused on the telephone. "You hired an ex-girlfriend?" Jessi observed, astounded that the question escaped her lips.

His eyes drifted up to her face, smoldering by the time they burned into hers. "She's a good engineer," he said. "But it isn't working out."

"She still cares about you," Jessi said. "I could tell when she was here."

"It has been over for a long time," he murmured.

"Kale…" His name burned on the end of her tongue. The conversation was creating a picture of him living twelve year's worth of broken relationships, loving and leaving, tasting and touching and seducing, and then moving on. Always moving on.

He dropped to his haunches and swung her chair around so that he was in front of her, his hands on the arms of her chair. He spoke as if he had been listening to her thoughts and wanted to explain, but he merely murmured her name, "Jessi…" and couldn't seem to hook on to the words he intended to deliver. Finally, he said softly, "There's no one else."

She assumed then that she was only *the next one,* that his attraction to her was something as dark and inevitable as the destruction bearing down upon them from the angry sky. He had wanted her but would give her no hold over him. Somehow, his wanting her was linked relentlessly to their shared past, to his anger with the Caldwell sisters, to his frustrated longing for her as an innocent youth and his savage instincts as a virile and potent man to possess her as he had failed to do in their youthful relationship.

How long would she hold his interest? How much would he hurt her when he moved on? She didn't want to believe his attraction to her was such a base involvement, but she was forced to recognize with dawning clarity that his feelings for her had nothing to do with love.

Even if he did love her a little, he would never marry a

woman who couldn't give him the children he wanted. It was an ache she had always before minimized because she had Amanda.

Jessi choked on the thought of how she would feel when he finally exorcised her from his life. *If* she let him into her life in an intimate relationship.

"Don't," she warned, forcing false strength into her voice. "We too are history."

He studied her face in silence. Behind the desire in his eyes, there burned an anger of long standing.

He rose slowly, and turned away from her, digging his hands into the pockets of his khaki shorts, wandering toward the window facing east where the ceiling of clouds was still innocuously pale gray and merely dreary.

"You're right," he replied quietly. "But our history is now current, isn't it? Revived. Renewed. Without a conclusion."

The silence between them hung as heavy as the humid stillness outside, expectant, warning of hidden shadows and powerful forces beyond their control.

She watched him standing impeccably still, not moving a muscle, as though he were frozen in time, completely withdrawn from her and the world around them.

He turned to her slowly and said, as if he were absently finishing a sentence, "And with a present, maybe even a future."

"I don't understand any of this," she told him softly, but he did not respond. He did not move. "Simply go home, and don't come back. Send someone else to do the on-site work." It seemed a simple enough solution, as much as it agonized her.

"It's too late for that, and you know it," he replied. "I was inside you last night, Jessi. Not all the way, and God only knows how we managed to stop when we did, but neither of us can deny we were making love. That we didn't complete what we started doesn't make it less real."

He turned his head so that their eyes met. "Only damned frustrating," he added.

She felt the heat of embarrassment flow from prickles on her neck to the hotness in her face, and she turned away from him, burying her face in her hands, her elbows planted on her desktop.

"For both of us," he added, and she heard him moving toward the door.

She listened to him moving away slowly down the stairs. She knew he was getting the key, and as she watched out the window, she saw him with the rolls of blueprints under his arm walking slowly to the rental car. When he opened the door, he stopped and looked up at her in the window, although she knew he couldn't see her through the double layers of tinted glass.

While she watched him drive away, his words reverberated through the quiet space surrounding her. She felt a strange irony in that she had never found with Rollie the pleasure and excitement Kale inspired every time he touched her.

How on earth was she going to find the strength to prevent him from consummating their relationship when her mind was overwhelmed with anticipating their intimacy?

Eight

The violence of the storm tore shingles from three of the hangars and damaged two planes tied down on the far side of the field. It uprooted an old jack pine on the edge of the parking lot and broke a branch off a balm of Gilead, sending it like a lethal javelin through a window in the mechanics' shed.

When the wind, thunder and lightning had travelled on to the east and a soft rain was falling, Jessi surveyed her little empire, thankful the damage wasn't worse and frowning at the scattered branches and debris that littered the ground everywhere.

She donned a yellow slicker, pulled the hood around her face and walked the length of the runway, tossing debris off the tarmac onto the grass. She didn't anticipate planes to be landing for a while, but it was her policy to keep the runway open at all times. She tossed branches, shingles, boards, sticks, a tennis shoe, mismatched gloves, a battered cap and wet newspaper to the west side of the runway for pickup later.

Amanda came to the field just as she was returning to the

office. "I'm leaving for my class. I checked the float plane and everything's okay," she announced. "I finished my reading. My teacher's really going to be impressed. You know, Jessi, we should have a personal computer in the office here. You could save a lot of time."

She grinned at her niece. "I've been waiting for you to recommend one," she said.

"Do you mean it?" Amanda screeched. "Really?"

"I've been thinking about it," Jessi said. "Want to help me shop around?"

"Definite yes!"

"Did you fix yourself lunch?"

"Tuna sandwich and an apple. I'm going to wait for the bus now."

Jessi gave her raincoated charge a hug and watched her trot across the parking lot to the road where she would sit and wait in the tiny two-person shed that stood at the edge of the county highway. Rollie had built the shed with a window on the north side so that Amanda could watch for the bus. He had built it when Amanda was in first grade and staying at their house frequently. It protected her from the biting cold and arctic winds of winter, as was its intent, but it also sheltered her from rain during warm weather.

As she reached for the door of the office, her beeper sounded. She flicked the switch and dialed her coded number.

"Jessi, there's been a terrible accident at the bridge. Air evac needed to Cabot General Hospital in Minneapolis." Michelle Riley's familiar voice sent ripples of fear through her blood.

"Who?" she demanded, willing her heart not to slam through her chest.

"No names yet," Michelle reported. "Nobody local."

Not Kale! It couldn't be Kale!

"Nobody local" was usually a comforting report. But not today. Certainly not today.

Chaz was on call, but Jessi simply unhooked her beeper and

lay it on the counter to let Chaz know what she was doing. After jotting a quick note to ask that he look after Amanda, she ran to the helicopter.

Everything seemed to be in slow motion, like tiny delays between every movement, every lever and switch she turned and pressed and pulled. In reality, though, it was only minutes before the blades were thumping and she was pulling off the ground headed for the Point Six construction site.

She made a pass over the site, according to procedure, seeing the upturned faces and waving arms in a sea of yellow slickers and hard hats. She knew they heard the reverberating thumping and saw her as an angel of mercy coming to save a life. She hovered momentarily and lowered to the ground, killing the rotors before anyone ran into the blades. She was grateful the wind had slowed so that she could land easily.

Her heart raced with fear. Not Kale! It wouldn't be Kale! She felt a dry sob of apprehension escape. Please, she prayed, let him be whole.

Del Kaskey, a paramedic she knew well, ducked under the slowing blades to tell her again they were headed for Cabot General Hospital. "It's bad," he said.

She pressed her eyes closed, wishing she had not denied him, regretting they had not given themselves up to making love last night. It had been a precious opportunity, and she had fought it. Now, was he injured, dying? The image of his gravely injured body scorched the insides of her eyelids. Was it over then? Had she squandered their only chance to come together?

She let out a long, relieved breath when the passenger door opened and someone was helping Kale out of a slicker and hard hat. Seeing him whole left her wanting to throw herself into his arms. It didn't matter that he looked worried and stunned. He wasn't the critically injured one.

When he saw her in the pilot's seat, his expression changed to one of confusion, although she didn't give it much thought at the moment.

Del, with the help of another medic and a couple of doctors from the clinic, was there, moving quickly. They knew what to do. Their unconscious patient was strapped onto an elaborate gurney, intravenous bags attached. They headed for the wide side door, which Jessi opened just before they reached it.

One of the doctors shouted the hospital name to her. "I know weather's bad. I hope you can make it," he said. "Take the engineer, too."

She looked down at the patient. It was Curt Burness, but she almost didn't recognize him. His skin was gray-white except where it seeped dark red blood. She saw the spilled and splattered blood on the blankets and cloths around him, and the dark red plastic sack alongside a clear one dripping into his arm.

She peeked under the top blanket to see the bulky life-saving body suit the medics had put him into. Her eyes met Del's. Their communication was silent but eloquent. The suit was used only in extreme cases, when there were extensive injuries and it was a long shot that the patient would even make it to the hospital.

The weather still wasn't good. She couldn't even guarantee she could get him there.

"If I can't get through, can I take him to Duluth?"

"Don't waste your time. He needs special surgery. There'll be a specialist waiting at Cabot," Del said. "I'm going to try to keep him alive until we get there."

When she slipped into the pilot's seat, she noted that Kale was already strapped into the passenger seat. She gestured toward the headset he should wear so they could communicate without shouting.

"Kale, I wish you weren't here," she said. "The weather isn't good. We might not make it." She began the familiar ritual of checking and starting the aircraft. She thought he wanted to stay with Curt, and get a ride to Minneapolis.

He frowned at the suggestion, awkwardly adjusting his

headset. He sat in the white shirt and khaki shorts he had worn that morning, only now they were stained with mud and blood and there was a rip on one thigh. When she glanced at it, she saw a thin line of blood and the deep purple of a heavy bruise. She looked at his exotic face, haggard and pale in the darkened cockpit, pulled tight with strain.

She saw another swollen bruise and scab forming just above his temple, and when he lifted his hand to touch an earphone, there was a thick swath of gauze around his left arm where blood was already seeping through.

"You're hurt!" she cried, staring at him.

"I've been treated. I'm okay," he said, but his voice sounded strangled.

She lifted the chopper easily and headed south southeast, calling in her medevac flight plan. Even though the storm had passed, there was another front approaching the southern part of the state from the west. The clouds ahead of them were thunderheads with tricky updrafts and unpredictable horizontal winds. The ceiling was low. Too low.

She flew close over the treetops, her blades stirring wisps of clouds. "How's the patient?" she asked Del.

"Pretty shaky," came the reply.

"What happened, Kale?"

When he answered, his voice was weak and strained, his words slowly spoken. "Scaffolding. Collapse. Too much mud. Ran to warn. Got all but one. Burness caught under, pushed project manager out of way before…" He stopped to catch his breath. "Told them not to use scaffolding with rain coming. Foreman thought…knew better."

She wondered for a fleeting moment why someone hadn't stopped the foreman, but her overpowering concern was for Kale. "Don't talk anymore. Rest now," she advised. He ignored her in spite of his obvious weakness.

"Burness and I, on other side. Didn't know still using same scaffold. Damn him. Know-it-all." The last words came out huskily, hesitantly, his voice fading.

She glanced at him and saw that his head was bobbing forward and his eyes were closed. He was either falling asleep or semiconscious.

"Del," she called, alarmed.

"He's holding on," Del replied.

"Can you leave him for a minute? Our other passenger is unconscious," she cried, sickened by Kale's pallor and the wounds she could see.

"Don't worry. Doc gave him a heavy painkiller before you got there. He was unconscious when we found him. His arm needs stitches." Del paused a moment and then continued. "He's not just riding along, Jessi. He's a patient. Damn fool should be on a stretcher with that head wound."

"Anything I should watch for?" she asked.

"I'll check on him periodically."

Her heart was racing. What if his injuries were worse than thought? What if he slipped into a coma, or his arm bled profusely and he lost too much blood? What if he didn't survive? What if Kale Noble died in her helicopter? With his injuries, she could stop in Virginia or Duluth and he would be taken care of. Shouldn't she know if he was in some kind of danger?

She lay her palm against his forehead and pushed his bobbing head back until it rested against the back of the seat. She cupped his cheek and ran her hand over his neck. There was blood on his shirt collar and down the front of the shirt, a wide ribbon of it dried into the fabric, covering his breast pocket.

She looked at the dark swollen place on his head and saw that it was growing worse. His eye was swelling shut. And a thick trickle of dark red blood was oozing out and running down the side of his face.

She fought tears. To see him like this—powerful, indomitable Kale, helpless and bleeding.

"Got an ice pack back there?" she asked.

"Sure, there's one in my kit."

"Hand it up. I'll hold it on his head."

Kale's hand came up to catch the ice pack. "I'm just... resting," he said with effort, wincing when Del slapped it onto his palm and he pressed it gingerly to his head. His eyes remained closed as he leaned back against the seat. "My parents don't know about Amanda yet," he whispered. "You tell them...if something happens...."

"Just fly the chopper, Jessi." Del's anxious voice reached her through the earphones. "Noble's going to be all right."

"His head...it's bleeding again. His eye is swelling shut," she choked.

"He's going to be okay," he replied. Then she saw him moving between their seats and inspecting Kale's wound. "Looks like you're going to need both hands to get us through that mess."

He was right to be concerned. The ceiling was only a few hundred feet over the ground at best, and it was a thick mass of dark gray clouds that threatened to punch them out of the sky.

She thought about some of the air evac agencies in the metropolitan area. Pilots were deliberately not told the nature of an emergency so that they wouldn't take chances. Well, she did know the nature of the emergency, personally knew the people injured, and she was damn well taking chances. She couldn't *not* make the effort.

She was watching ahead closely, calling to airports with radio contact along the way, zigging and zagging according to ground reports. Passing over St. Cloud, the ceiling raised and they climbed, but then the tornado watch started. Thank God it wasn't a warning. She'd have had to go to ground.

She scanned the low horizon for funnels anyway, and she watched the terrain for high towers and blinking strobes. She listened to reports, and after an hour she was finally within range of the Twin Cities aviation services.

She was directed straight to the Cabot General helipad. The threatening thunderstorm struck just as she was landing, tossing the chopper around and forcing her to make three attempts before she finally landed on her target. Only two wheels were on the cement pad when she finally shut down the engine, but her passengers were safe, and she was immediately surrounded by many helping hands.

Burness was still alive. Kale was unconscious, or asleep. Hospital employees, their white uniforms covered with clear plastic rain gear, pulled him out of the seat while he groaned in protest, lay him on a stretcher and pushed him quickly indoors. Burness's gurney was pulled out, the wheels unlatched, and he was also pushed hurriedly indoors.

She longed to run alongside Kale, but there was her chopper to tend to. Several maintenance workers came out in rain gear to help her.

When she found her way to the emergency room, she was carrying the wet slicker against her khaki shorts and sleeveless shirt. She was too distracted to realize she was making a mess of her clothes or to think about her hair, frizzed out of control with wind and rain.

The first person she saw was Londa, and then Mike, who was holding her within the curve of a protective arm while the tears pooled in her eyes. She looked upon Jessi with contempt. "Two hours it took you!" she charged. "It never takes two hours! What were you doing? He might have died while you fooled around getting him here!"

Jessi, strained with fear for Kale, exhausted from a restless night and two hours of incredible tension, merely stared at the woman, mouth agape. She had done well just getting them through. All during the hundred-and-fifty mile ordeal, she had been advised time and again to turn back or to land and wait out the weather, and she had refused. She had flown into and under and around clouds that had brought lumps into her throat, gone miles out of her way to get around nature's violence, and she had persisted and got them here. And this woman was accusing her of, what? Dawdling? Of incompetence?

Del appeared suddenly out of nowhere and placed himself before Kale's small entourage, hands on his hips, his blond hair plastered to his head, his tall, wide Nordic body stiff with anger and fatigue, his high-boned Scandinavian features drawn into a fierce scowl.

"I don't know who you are, lady," he threatened, "but you sure have a lot of apologizing to do to Jessi Morris." He pointed his index finger at Jessi, his eyes fastened fiercely on the slender blonde before him. "She risked her life to get us here. She flew through weather that sent every other damn aircraft in the state to ground, and she ignored at least twenty warnings to land or turn back. She damn well did the finest and bravest job of flying I've ever seen, and I've been a paramedic for eleven years. If it weren't for her, Curt Burness would be dead instead of in surgery right now."

A nurse poked her head out of a curtain and told him to shush. Then she looked from one woman to the other. "He's asking for Jessi."

It was Londa's turn to stare in astonishment, which soon turned into a glare. She ignored Del, who was waiting for her to apologize.

"That's me," Jessi said quietly, moving quickly toward the curtain through which the nurse was partially revealed.

Jessi slid alongside the gurney where Kale lay, one eye swollen shut, one side of his forehead a massive bruise. A physician was preparing to sew up a vicious gash on his forearm. His other eye was partially open, held there with great effort, it appeared, and on his mouth was a weak grin.

"Jessi," he whispered, obviously capable of no more than that at the moment. She leaned closely over him and gently brushed his hair back.

"Oh, Kale, I was so worried about you," she cried softly.

"You got us here. I knew you would. You must be a hell of a pilot." His words were whispered and slow as he labored to speak. Then the smile faded and his eyes fluttered. "Jessi?" he pleaded so softly she had to put her ear to his mouth.

"Yes, Kale?"

"Kiss me, Jessi," he said.

She lifted her face to see his eye close and then flutter open momentarily and close again. She leaned down and kissed his lips lightly, tenderly.

When she raised her face, she saw a smile barely twitch at the corners of his mouth, and then he was still, and she knew he had slipped once more into a drugged sleep.

"He's going to be all right," the physician said, smiling quickly, intent upon his task. "Are you a, uh, relative?"

"No," she replied. "I'm his...pilot."

The man pursed his lips, obviously amused. "I see," he said finally, beginning the stitching on Kale's arm.

The nurse gestured for her to leave, which she did. Reluctantly.

Once outside the curtain, Jessi saw that Londa's face was buried in Mike's chest. Mike was looking helpless and bewildered, and Del was scowling at Londa.

"They're patching him up," Jessi announced, which brought Londa's tear-stained face whirling toward her.

"We've been waiting here for over an hour. And when he comes in they won't let us see him." She inhaled deeply as though gearing up for another confrontation, but merely collapsed in a sob.

"He passed out in the middle of our conversation in the chopper," Jessi said quietly. "He just wanted to finish what he was saying before we left for Kenross."

Londa's shaky voice tried to threaten. "I intend to file a complaint with your superiors."

Del and Jessi exchanged a weary look. "Del is a volunteer," Jessi explained. "And he did a fine job. He kept Curt Burness alive when no one thought Curt would make it."

"A *volunteer*?" Londa was visibly aghast. "Not even a professional?"

"Let's sit, Londa," Mike suggested, obviously embarrassed by her outburst.

He led her away. Her voice drifted back to Jessi and Del. "I don't intend to let this go unreported."

Jessi was grateful that the weather was going to keep them grounded for the next several hours, for it gave her a reason to hang around and keep an eye on Kale.

The nurse came out half an hour later to say that Mr. Noble would be moved to his hospital room soon. She gave them the number. Jessi said they would pass on the information to Mr. Noble's employees who waited in the lounge.

Del offered to do so, while Jessi continued to stand in the middle of the emergency treatment room, watching the nurse and physician moving swiftly, leaning over Kale's still form behind the white curtains. She could see the shadows of their heads moving, and their hands, and then she saw the nurse place an oxygen mask over Kale's face. A sliver of fear raced through her, and she found herself fighting an urge to tear through the curtain and demand an explanation. Was he worse?

She stared, frozen, studying each gesture and movement seen in silhouette behind the curtain. And she listened. But the noises behind the other curtains and their subdued voices made eavesdropping impossible.

Nearing panic, she slipped through the curtain just as the nurse was hooking up a heart monitor. There was a thin cord attached to a white plastic circle on his chest. Jessi gasped aloud. "What happened?"

The physician rose from his chair and stretched his neck backward, lifting first one shoulder and then the other. "It's all right," he said, finally looking at her. "Just a precaution. We don't want to take any chances with that nasty head wound, so we're going to monitor him for twenty-four hours."

"But the oxygen..."

"He has two broken ribs. His prognosis is excellent," he said. "But he's in a lot of pain. And he will continue to be for some time with these injuries. I'd say he's a very lucky man. If any of his injuries had been a little worse, we wouldn't be so optimistic.''

''I'm sorry to intrude,'' she murmured. ''Just take good care of him. Take all the precautions you can think of....''

''It's his treatment we're most concerned with,'' he said, smiling warmly. ''And you seem to have a special knack for providing the most effective healing. We can't compete with that.'' His face broke into a broad grin, and she reddened, knowing he was referring to the kiss she had bestowed on Kale.

''A lot of good I did. He just passed out afterward,'' she reminded.

''You don't know how much you did,'' the doctor corrected. ''You must be very special to him,'' he added, striding to Kale's side to check his patient one last time. He turned to her again before leaving. ''Very special,'' he said again.

Nine

A pale, unconscious Kale let out a short groan. His head jerked and then settled again. Jessi moved from the chair at his bedside and leaned over him, brushing a gentle hand over his hair. His lips moved without sound, as if he struggled to communicate.

Then his head flew to the other side and he winced. "Paul!" he cried in a weak voice filled with panic. "Paul!"

"It's all right, Kale," she soothed, leaning close to his face, her hand on his thick black hair. "It's all right."

"An accident! He's hurt!"

"Yes, yes, but everything's going to be all right," she soothed, her heart leaping, her stomach churning. He was in another time and place, where she, too, had often traveled in darkness and pain.

"His back is hurt," Kale cried.

"Everything's going to work out, Kale," she whispered and brushed his lips lightly with hers, leaving behind a kiss from which she sucked the sweetness that had been Kale as a teenager.

"Hold me, Jessi," he whispered. "I need you."

She stopped, knowing the words were spoken by an adolescent to a fifteen-year-old girl, both of them innocents, in another life, a long time ago. "I need you, too, Kale," she whispered, pretending for a moment that she was still that young girl.

How many times over the years had she dreamed she could go back and change what was to come?

"Everything's going to be all right, Kale," she whispered as she had fantasized so many times when she thought about how she would have changed the following sequence of events. "Everything's going to be…okay," she lied. But it wasn't really a lie, was it? Not when his conscious mind couldn't hear her. "And so are we."

As if they could backtrack and do it over, her reassuring words slipped out. "We're going to weather this and be happy together. We have each other. Without bitterness, without terrible mistakes, without recriminations and guilt."

Her words caught on a sob before she went on to say what she had wished thousands of times when the sickening pain had overwhelmed her, and even in later years when the unwelcome memories merely haunted. "We're going to love each other forever. We're going to be together, drawing strength from each other, forgiving, trusting and loving, and we aren't going to let anyone take that away from us, Kale."

Her voice gave out with a choke then, even though she was doing no more than low whispering, dreaming aloud.

"Thank God," he sighed. "Stay, Jessi…" His voice trailed off and his head was still, his lips and eyelids relaxed and immobile again. His features were peaceful, the harsh lines softened. She saw for the first time the teenager's face matured to manhood without bitterness.

He hadn't really heard her, had he? Of course he hadn't.

He was unconscious, rendered insensate by anesthetics. He would not remember any of it when he awoke.

She sank into the chair alongside his bed. He had loved her then. And she had certainly loved him, although she had told herself over the years it couldn't have been anything real or lasting, for she was only fifteen, and she always thought of it as being a kind of puppy love, the sort of premature thing that happened to children when they went through puberty and wanted to be adult and experience adult feelings. She had told herself countless times since then that it was a kind of preparation for falling in love as an adult, a sweet longing, a romantic obsession, a gentle prelude to the passions of adulthood, something intended to pass harmlessly and become honeyed memory.

Now she saw this righteous approach for what it was, a superficial balm to soothe the wretched effects of her profound regret.

Her sad reverie was cruelly interrupted when Mike brought Londa into the room and she let escape a muted shriek. "I can't bear to look at him," Londa cried, turning her back and burying her face in her hands. Mike was quick to comfort her. "Can't they bandage his face?" she demanded. "Cover it with something so that he doesn't look so terrible? And what's that up his nose? It's repulsive."

"Oxygen, Londa. It's just oxygen," Mike explained.

"Whatever for?"

"I'm not sure. I think they give it to everyone who is unconscious," he replied, rubbing a palm on her spine.

She looked over her left shoulder at Jessi in the chair. "Why are you here?"

"Del is checking on Curt Burness. I'm sitting with Kale. We can't leave for a while," Jessi said.

"Oh," Londa said in a small voice. "Yes, the weather."

"Let me take you home, Londa," Mike suggested quietly.

"I don't think I should just leave him here," she said in a voice Jessi was hard pressed not to call a whine.

"You can't do anything for him while he's out anyway, and he does have company. The pilot will stay for a while," Mike said, casting a glance at Jessi, who nodded in agreement.

"Will they call us if he wakes up?" she asked as if Jessi weren't there in the same room.

"Yes, I'll leave them a number."

"I think…I think I'll just go back to work," she said, walking slowly out the door, not looking back at Kale. She was saving face by leaving, Jessi decided. Not only was she already rejected as a lover, but she had made a fool of herself in front of all of them.

"The number…" Jessi reminded Mike.

He pulled a mechanical pencil out of a plastic holder in his shirt pocket and wrote on a small pad in tiny perfect letters the telephone number at Noble Engineering. "Are you an artist?" she asked.

"An engineer," he corrected, smiling weakly, carefully returning the fine-leaded mechanical pencil to the plastic pen holder in his pocket, and tucking the tiny pad neatly behind it. He folded the little sheet expertly, exactly in half, and handed it to Jessi. "You'll call if he asks for, uh, any of us?" He glanced warily toward Londa's retreating back.

"Yes, of course," she replied and watched him catch up with the tall, obnoxious blonde.

She looked again at Kale lying in peaceful oblivion on the stark white bed. She doubted she could have explained her feelings. She didn't know why tears were threatening to choke her, or why she had an unbearable impulse to caress and hold him, to touch him and stroke him, to run her fingers through his hair and adjust the sheet a fraction of an inch higher. Neither did she know why it touched her so deeply to see him helpless, to feel his relentless life force dormant, to note his dark skin incongruous against the mocking white of crisp sanitized sheets.

She lightly grasped his hand, and put a finger on his pulse just to feel him being alive. What am I to him now, she wondered. Am I part of the past that haunts him? Am I merely unfinished business? Physically desirable enough for a passing dalliance? Am I another romantic mistake for him? A rash decision? A detour in his life's path?

When he woke up, she intended to tell him it would not work, that she could not bear to be any of those things in his life. But she knew she would never say it. Maybe, she mused, he would not even want her when he was clearheaded and healed. Maybe his interest would already have passed by then.

The memory of the night they had come together on her front porch intruded again as though it had happened some time in the past and become a part of their former life together. She trembled at the reminder that it had been less than twenty-four hours ago. Only last night she had felt his powerful body pressed against her, felt him between her thighs, making love to her. She relived once again how much she had wanted him then, and how lost she had been in the rapture of his skilled attentions.

But he hadn't completed the act.

She thought about the kind of woman he would marry, beautiful, tall and slender, educated, bright, well-dressed, and able to have his children.

She thought of them dancing together, attending a theatre performance, or the symphony, or a country club dinner dance, relaxing on a Grand Cayman beach she would likely never see. Or proudly attending school programs where beautiful sons and daughters performed. None of it was familiar to her. All she knew were airplanes and small-town life in the north woods.

She was the antithesis of what she pictured for him, her earthy body too rounded and unfashionable, unable even to reproduce, her social experience abysmal, her hair frizzed like unloomed wool, her clothes smelling of aviation fuel. When was the last time she'd had a bottle of cologne? Years ago. She couldn't remember the name of it.

Jessica Caldwell Morris belonged in her Up North rustic

cottage, crawling into bed at night scented with wood smoke rather than bath salts.

She was his summer diversion.

And what was he to her?

There was no lasting place for him in her life either. They had matured into disparate worlds.

She felt an overwhelming urge to flee, to release the chopper and head for home in spite of the weather, to escape forever the sight and touch of the handsomest man in the world lying immobile in a hospital bed.

Yet, when he flung his head to the side and back again and grimaced, she was instantly leaning over him, reaching out to soothe and calm him when he called out.

His restlessness progressed, telling her he was coming out of his drugged state. Suddenly he said, slightly slurred but easily understandable, "You wouldn't leave me, would you, Jessi?"

"I'm here, Kale," she whispered. "I'm here. I'll stay with you."

"Don't leave me...." he ordered softly, his voice fading to a murmur, his body relaxing once again.

"I won't," she whispered, knowing it was a lie if she spoke as that teenager twelve years before when she had left him without a word and never seen him again.

This time, however, she was promising to stay by his bedside, and that she could do, however little atonement it might be for leaving him years before as a confused, disappointed and emotionally wounded girl.

Eventually, she slept, awakened by Del who reported that Curt Burness's surgery had been successful. The man was stable and his condition was upgraded from critical to serious.

"Looks as though we saved another one, Jess," he said, grinning.

"You kept him alive," she reminded him. "I only flew the chopper."

"Noble doesn't look so good," he said.

"He'll be all right. All this equipment is a precaution because of the head wound," she explained.

"Looks pretty harmless when he's asleep," he observed. "Why oxygen...?"

"The doctor said something about broken ribs," she reported.

"Ah, yes," he agreed, nodding. "He was probably breathing too shallow because of the pain."

"He's been dreaming," she said.

"Out of his head?"

"Into the past."

"It happens. Want to get some dinner?" Reaching for her hand, he coaxed, "C'mon, you probably haven't eaten all day." After only a short hesitation and an awareness that her stomach was begging, she agreed.

When they returned to Kale's room after dinner, he was groggily half-awake and his enormous bruise was loosely covered with neat layers of gauze wrapped at an angle that partially covered his left eye.

When he saw Jessi and Del arrive, he frowned at her, as though trying to focus on something that was eluding him.

Del walked purposefully around the side of the bed. "Curt Burness is recovering," he said. "His surgery was successful and his condition upgraded."

Kale stared at him in some confusion, and then closed his visible eye and nodded. "Good," he murmured.

"I think I'll call for the weather report," Del said, backing toward the door.

"Jessi," Kale called, his voice faint, his good eye closed.

She moved slowly.

"I dreamed..." Kale started, his good eye fluttering open. His voice was so soft, she had to lean close to hear. "I thought, when I woke up, it was a long time ago. And everything was different." He opened his palm where his wrist and elbow were strapped to a board so that his intravenous needles would not be disturbed by his movements.

She slid her hand into his and he gripped it, although the pressure from him was weak. "You were dreaming, Kale," she said softly, squeezing his hand.

"Come back tomorrow. Talk to me," he whispered.

"I can't promise. If the weather lifts, we'll have to leave," she explained.

"Pray for a storm," he replied, his voice barely a whisper, his good eye closing.

She watched his face, watched him struggle to remain awake, saw his distress and confusion, and his weariness.

He blinked. "Is it too late?" he whispered slowly.

She stared at him, speechless, bewildered and questioning. She reminded herself that he hadn't been exactly coherent or alert since arriving at the hospital.

He seemed to be in the present. And still, she couldn't make sense of his question.

"Touch me," he whispered.

"Touch you? Where?"

"Anywhere. Your fingers…"

She cupped his chin in her palm, feeling the light stubble against her skin. She ran her fingertips over his bottom lip. "Sleep," she coaxed him softly. "I'll be back in the morning."

"Promise." The word was barely a whisper, more a movement of his lips and a small puff of air against her fingers.

"I promise," she said.

Ten

His first awareness was that he hurt from his head to his knees, and so he willed himself to be still, deadly still. He was good at that.

His next thought was that he had been hurt in a needless accident. And…Curt Burness? Had Curt survived? Had the helicopter made it in time? Vaguely, he remembered the tall, blond Swede telling him that Curt had survived surgery and was recovering. Or had he dreamed it?

Third was the realization that Jessi was sleeping somewhere not too distant, and if the sun was indeed going to shine, then she would be leaving promptly, returning in her mercy ship to her home in the north.

It was important that she not leave. His thoughts were hazy and confusing, but he remembered it was important.

He was aware of the unnatural bulk over the left side of his forehead where the skin felt pulled inordinately tight and an unrelenting pain throbbed. When he tried to touch it with his right hand, he recalled his arm was attached to a board and tubes were emanating from his arm into an I.V. sack suspended on chrome poles alongside his bed. When he attempted to move his left hand to investigate his head, a sharp pain brought tears to his eyes and a hoarse gasp to his lips. When he gasped, he inhaled sharply and another pain struck him in the right side. Broken ribs. He remembered vaguely the doctor in the emergency room working on his arm and telling him that he had two cracked ribs.

Nothing life-threatening, he had been told. But painful. They were right about that. Painful it was. Unless he remained perfectly still. And then the pain was minimal.

Jessi was coming back.

It was important, but why did he feel a thrill of hope that she was coming back?

Then it came to him clearly, like an impressionistic vision—the dream. But it wasn't a dream, it was a remembrance from his youth, of Jessi comforting him after Paul's accident, of Jessi talking softly to him after Charlotte had left, of Jessi telling him Paul was going to watch over them, and everything was going to be all right.

Jessi hadn't left him.

It was a brand-new scenario, and she hadn't left him. An innocent young Jessi said she loved him and wouldn't leave him.

None of the bad things had happened.

She had stayed with him, and…and then, what? The bitterness had never come.

The loneliness had never been.

The betrayals had not happened.

She had warmed his heart, returned his love, stayed by him, touching him gently with her fingertips, kissing him softly on the lips, whispering tenderly into his mouth.

She had made the pain disappear.

She promised to stay. She promised not to leave him. She touched him. She loved him.

She was his mate, the other half of him, the softer half, the warmer half, perhaps the stronger half, in some ways, the part of him that kept the beast at bay, the part of his spirit that reflected the gentleness that was so elusive when he thought of life without her.

Twelve bleak and empty years had been but a capricious nightmare, and it was over now.

The bad years, the bad times, the anguish and pain and loneliness had not happened, had never needed to happen, because she had been there to keep them away, had been there to love him, to be a part of him, to soothe him and gentle him, to prove she loved him and wanted nothing else but to keep her place, attached to him in a way that could never be undone.

The mystical nature of his experience was beautiful and nurturing, but it was wrenching, too, for although it was as real as the daylight altering the color of his hospital room, it was slipping away from him.

He wanted desperately to hang on to it, the new, wonderful, peaceful reality filled with joy and love. He had known last night it was real. He had felt her there, had felt her lips and her hands, heard her words, her promise, as though all that had happened in twelve years had been but a dream and the new truth was that she had stayed.

But he was in his hospital room. He had been injured in Kenross, and Jessi, a twenty-eight-year-old Jessi, who had been married for over eight years to another man, had flown him to Minneapolis in her helicopter.

His eyes burned with the loss.

His body was racked with a pain a thousand times worse than his physical wounds, for it was the undoing of the oneness he had thought for a time to be real. And for the few hours the new truth had been real, he had fused her to him so completely he could no longer tell where he began and she began, and so the reality was more painful than it ever had been when she had simply betrayed him, gone away and never come back.

The events were unclear, mixed up and shadowy. Everything that had happened after he climbed into the passenger seat of her helicopter became a part of another world, inexorably tied to this existing world and to his past, and tied with unbreakable bonds to Jessi Caldwell, as she had been then, and, across an empty void, as she was now.

It was as though a giant spiritual trickster had invaded his soul at its moment of ultimate vulnerability and played out this great and wonderful travesty that now agonized him by its very nonexistence.

For a short time it had been real, so real he couldn't bear the thought of returning to the life he had built for himself over the last twelve years.

He finally remembered her leaning over him, touching his lips. He had begged, damn his weak soul, *begged* her to come back, to make a promise not to leave him. That was all he remembered.

She wasn't coming.

She had promised, but once again, she had left him.

In the quiet stillness of early dawn he grieved silently in his hospital bed, and when the nurse came in and asked if he wanted something for his pain, he replied that yes, but only a little, just in case Jessi came back as she had promised.

Later in the morning Jessi visited his room, hoping he would be lucid and capable of conversation.

Instead he seemed in a deeper state of unconsciousness than he had been the night before. She spoke to him quietly, but he did not respond.

She sat with him until nine o'clock, then Del reminded her they both had other responsibilities in Kenross and there was no more reason to delay their departure.

She left Kale with great reluctance, dawdling at his bedside, touching his hand and his face, wanting to taste his lips, wanting to stay with him and watch over him. She had never felt so close to him.

She had never before felt that he needed her as he did now. It caused an inexplicable pain in her abdomen to leave him alone and helpless in a cold white hospital bed, injured and unconscious.

Jessi was full of the consequence of leaving him, feeling that in some way she was failing him. She kissed him, pressing her lips to his soft mouth.

But finally, she turned away and walked from the room, and with Del in the passenger seat, she flew the chopper back to Kenross through clear blue cloudless skies.

Chaz and Amanda were waiting for her. She had called them before leaving Minneapolis, then again on the chopper radio when she was still a few miles from the Kenross airport. She leaped to the ground and let Chaz gas the engine.

"Sure glad Burness is doing all right," Chaz said.

"He's recovering well," she said. "So is Kale, I think."

"Was Kale hurt, too?" Amanda cried. "I didn't know Kale was hurt!"

"Head wound, couple of broken ribs, cuts and bruises. He'll be fine," she told her, smiling. "He was sleeping when I left the hospital."

"He's in the hospital, too?"

"He'll be fine," she reassured Amanda.

Jessi breathed in deeply and looked around the field, at the hangars and planes and her office building. She let her eyes wander over the sky, checking out the clouds and the wind. It was a relief to be home, to be beyond Kale's magnetic pull, to have her feet on the ground, solid and secure, to be with the people who had become her family. At least, that was what she said to herself.

"I'm going to run home and change clothes," she said.

"Yeah, you look kinda wrinkled," Amanda observed. "What do you think's going to happen to the bridge construction?"

"It will probably continue on schedule. Mr. Burness has a

project manager and Kale has an assistant,'' she said, walking toward the sidewalk.

She trotted across the parking lot, past the restaurant, and took the steps onto her front porch at a run. As soon as she entered the house, she felt his presence, as if he were about to step into the room from the hall, or sitting at the dining room table poring over blueprints.

She wandered to the dining area where she found her table still hosting the work he had left there when he went to the bridge site the day before. Plans in neat rolls sat tidily in a row on one end of the table. His briefcase was on the floor alongside the table, and she mentally retraced their steps, realizing that Chaz must have retrieved the rental car and Kale's briefcase from the bridge site.

When she walked into the guest bedroom, she found his suit hanging in the closet, a wilted white shirt hanging on the back of a chair, his athletic bag on the floor by the bed, his shaving kit on the dresser. She ran her hands over his things, not wanting to think about how close he had come to never returning. When would he come back, she wondered? Or would he ever come back?

Mike would probably take over his role in the bridge project. Certainly, Mike would have to take over for a while anyway. Kale would be in no shape to travel until his body healed.

She moved his things from the dining room into the guest room and closed the door. She didn't think it was good for her mental health to feel his presence so keenly in her house, not when she knew her next major self-preserving effort must be to minimize his presence in her life.

Settling into routine was her first order of business, and she slipped into it with decided fervor, in her home, in her relationships and in her business. She called the hospital the next morning, but learned Kale had just been discharged.

Five days later Chaz informed her that Noble's secretary had called and Mike, his assistant, was reserving the rental car for the next day.

"Did she say how he is?"

There was no need to explain who Jessi meant. "Home from the hospital, coming into the office this afternoon, she said," Chaz reported.

The next day, her heart jerked a little when she saw the Noble Engineering Bonanza ease onto the runway, even knowing Kale was not aboard. She met Mike in the office and handed him the car keys, asking about Kale's health. She had his bag, his suit, his briefcase and the blueprints for Mike.

"Stubborn man. He's back at his desk. Looking a little better than when last you saw him," Mike said with a humorless laugh. "But pretty grim."

"And have you seen Curt Burness?"

"Yes, we met in his hospital room last night. His wife is staying with him. He's much better. He expects to be back on the job in another week or so."

"That's incredible."

"Yes, it is. The project is going ahead, with a couple minor adjustments," Mike reported.

"Such as the removal of the foreman?"

"Oh, so you know about that?"

"Everyone does," she told him, wondering how he could think it would remain a secret on a job site in a small town.

Mike returned early the next week and again a few days later, and then, during the first week of August, when they were expecting him, it was Kale who stepped stiffly down from the wing of the plane. When Jessi saw him, she gasped and suppressed the impulse to run to him and throw herself into his arms.

The left side of his forehead was slightly marred by a pink scar where stitches had been, and his left eye was a little puffy. His face appeared more deeply lined, which she assumed was caused by a weight loss during his recovery.

What startled her when she met him at the counter was the wariness in his eyes and the business in his voice.

"Hello, Jessica Morris," he said, his dark eyes boring

through her. It was the first time he had acknowledged that her name was no longer Caldwell.

Bewildered at his distance and the uncertainty in his face, she asked finally, "How are you, Kale?"

"Better," he said and held out his hand for the key.

"Is the project going well?" she inquired, reaching into the drawer for the car key.

"Remarkably well considering the problems we've had," he replied, as if she were a stranger.

She dropped the key into his palm. "Have a nice day," she said, studying him, puzzled by his behavior, although, when she remembered the first few times she had seen him this summer, she realized he was considerably softened by comparison.

When the door closed behind him, she felt like crying, and then she felt like lashing out at him. She had lost him.

Well, wasn't that what she wanted? To get him out of her personal life? Of course, that was what she wanted. Hadn't she dreaded his persistence and his wanting her?

Now that something had happened to turn him off, she should be thankful. He was obviously as done with her as she wanted to be with him.

It was a relief. Yes, it certainly was a relief. There was nothing more to worry about. She could get on with things, the way they had always been. She could finally put Kale Noble out of her mind.

Why did the thought leave her feeling grievously deprived?

What had changed, she wondered, since the last time she saw him? It was Jessi he had wanted to kiss in his hospital room. It was Jessi he had asked to see in the emergency room. It was Jessi he had asked to come back, not to leave him, to touch him.

Who was this man who treated her like a stranger? And why? Why?

Don't probe, she warned herself. It's what you wanted.

Don't question it. But she did. Many times during the afternoon.

When he returned, she studied him closely and she saw something else in his face.

It was pain.

Something, or someone, had hurt him. She wondered who. She wondered what had happened to him since she had seen him last.

She started to push the form across the counter at him but held her fingers on it instead. She watched his pen poised to sign. When she continued to keep the form from him, he looked up, questioning.

"Why are you treating me like this?"

He flinched at her question and tightened his mouth as if the answer was too difficult.

"The last time I saw you—"

"You promised to come back in the morning," he interrupted. "It was a promise. I remembered it." His voice was quiet, his forearms on the countertop. "I never saw you again." His voice had become a whisper. "Did you come back as you promised?"

She knew now what gnawed at him. He didn't want to accuse her of breaking a promise she might not have broken. She smiled. "I came back, sat for an hour and had to leave. You were asleep."

He studied her, his eyes warming, a slight smile itching at his lips. He nodded almost imperceptibly several times. "I'm coming back tomorrow, and I'm staying a week. I've managed to get a room at the motel down the road. Will it inconvenience you if I rent your car for the week?" His voice was soft, as if he were proposing something seductive.

"I'll work around it," she told him, studying his dark eyes.

When he was heading for the door, an irresistible urge to stop him prompted her to say, "I called the hospital the next morning but you were gone." She neither understood nor liked the strange desperation that seized her.

His pace slowed. He stopped, and then he continued, pulling upon the door. Suddenly he stopped again and closed the door. He dropped the briefcase and strode to her, slipping behind the counter. He was looming over her before she realized his intentions, and he had her chin gently in the grip of his hand.

She closed her eyes because she knew they were about to get teary and she didn't want him to see what he was doing to her. She didn't want him to know he had touched something deep within her. What a fool she was to want him so.

"Were you waiting for me?" he questioned softly. "This isn't a game, is it? The stakes are too high this time. Open your eyes, Jessi, open them."

She opened them cautiously. His image was overwhelming, standing tall over her, his darkness like a portrait of masculine splendor. His other hand came up and slid around her neck, under her ear, to the back where it exerted a familiar pressure, pulling her face toward him.

His lips met hers with a crushing force, his one hand holding her head while his other slid down her back and pulled her against the full length of his body. For a matter of seconds, she resisted, but it seemed pointless, considering how much she wanted this from him. She felt the fullness of his groin pressing against her, and she felt his hips pushing to reach her, to give her his passion and create the friction that would escalate into full-blown lovemaking. She curled against him, accepting the tantalizing rhythm of his body.

She accepted his tongue stroking and caressing and possessing. She accepted all of him, and when he pulled his mouth away, she responded to the nips and bites he planted on her lips. He held her captive in his arms, telling her unmistakably what he wanted and when he wanted it, and she did not fight him. When his knee separated her legs, she complied.

"Now," he whispered into her mouth. "Now, Jessi."

"Someone might find us."

He backed her slowly to the doorway and into the storage room, then he slammed the door shut. He reached back and flipped a lock that was only used when the place was closed for the night.

Then he kneeled before her, unzipped her pants and pulled them down, underwear included. He unlaced her shoes and pulled them off. As she stepped out of her pants, he kissed her thighs, moving upward until he reached the tops of her legs. He pulled one thigh over his shoulder and flicked his tongue onto the sensitive bud so that she gasped and jerked and cried out in awe and shock.

And in that moment she was totally consumed, focused only on him and the intense pleasure of what he was doing to her. She grabbed his hair and flung her head back to gasp air into her lungs, but her excitement was so great she could barely catch her breath.

Soon he was standing before her, unbuckling his belt and freeing himself. He pulled her up against him and moved forward so that her backside rested on the worktable, and then he plunged into her, thrusting deep and sure, holding himself there. She heard herself yelp in ecstasy and she felt his groan as he buried his face in her hair and kissed her temple and her ear.

"Oh, Jessi," he moaned. "It's too good. You feel too good."

She tightened around him and felt him move slowly, in small thrusts, and heard him moan, which heightened her own sensation until she was caught in mindless rapture. She raised her knees and clasped her legs around him, lost to him and the feelings he stimulated. It was only the two of them, isolated in the universe, committed only to being a part of each other, of flying together to some nameless bright place where everything would explode into soft light and harmony, and she would be fulfilled.

They did fly together, and within seconds she felt the exquisite pressure of an imminent if strange explosion, and it frightened even as it pleasured her, so that her first instinct was to fight it. "Let it happen," he coaxed hoarsely in her ear, holding her so tightly she couldn't draw a full breath.

And she did. Let it happen. It was an explosion, and Kale placed his palm over her mouth to muffle her scream, and then he shuddered and pushed against her womb while he pumped into her.

Her legs fell powerless to the outside of his thighs and she let her head fall against the hardness of his chest. Still, he held her tightly, caressing her back and shoulders with his hands, holding her against his heaving body while he tried to breathe.

Even when his body slowed and relaxed, he continued to hold her against him and to stroke her back and shoulders. She felt a faint trembling deep inside him, and she wondered, with her return to consciousness, what was happening in him. Lovemaking, in her experience, ended promptly and completely after the climax. But she found it heavenly in his arms where she basked sated and happy. He could hold her as long as he liked, even though she didn't understand it.

Eventually, she moved her legs up again so that her knees clutched at his waist, and very slowly she felt him growing inside her, and gradually thrusting deeper. She inhaled sharply in shock and raised her face to his. She hadn't known a man could repeat himself so soon.

What she saw startled her, for his eyes were so soft and his lips were so full and loving. He cradled her, one hand coming up to caress her cheek, and then he kissed her with tenderness and passion, so slow and loving, she lost control of herself. While he kissed her, he pulled out of her and thrust again, as slowly and as tenderly as he kissed her.

Once again she was lost, taking flight instantly, hanging on to his hard body, grasping his shirt and then his neck, moving in a frenzy that overcame his languid rhythm, wild with a passion she had never before known, once again seeking the bright explosion, this time knowing it was there.

It ended too quickly, she thought, but couldn't help it or delay it or give a thought to anything else as wave after wave of pure pleasure gripped her body and soul and drove her over the edge of sanity. She was vaguely aware that Kale, too, had found release a second time, and once again, she collapsed and he held her tightly against him, his shirt now drenched with their perspiration.

She wanted to fall sleep against his chest until her bones reformed and she could stand on her own.

He slid his hands from around her and gripped her arms above her elbows. With great effort she raised her head and looked into his face, the lines of which were broken by a smile she had never seen before. She studied him in astonishment and a kind of glee.

"Jessi," he whispered, shaking his head in wonder. "I didn't know making love could be so…so much."

"You aren't suspicious anymore?" she asked without sense.

"I don't know what you do to me. I don't want to stop."

"You're a wonderful lover, Kale," she told him.

"This is just the beginning. Next time, I want you naked, in cool sheets, on a soft bed," he said.

"Next time?"

"Tomorrow night. I'm coming back tomorrow. I'll be here for a week, remember?"

"I just heard the outside door. I think someone is coming in," she told him, wide-eyed.

He backed up and scooped her clothes off the floor, handing them to her. "It's probably Phil, wondering what's keeping me," he said, tucking in his wet shirt, pulling his pants closed.

"I forgot about Phil," she wailed. "He's going to know what we've been doing."

"Yes, undoubtedly," he replied, grinning, running his hands through his hair as he headed for the door. With his fingers on the handle he turned back to see if she was presentable. She was slipping into her shoes, leaving her socks on the table.

He unlocked the door and opened it a crack to look out.

"I'll be out shortly," he said. "Wait in the plane." Then he silently closed the door again. He strode to her and ran his hands over the wet frizzed hair along her face. "You look like a little girl. I remember when you had freckles. I miss your freckles," he said, his eyes roaming fondly over her face and hairline.

"I think you'd better spend a little time in the ladies' room. You look like a woman who has just been ravished by a very hungry man."

He kissed her lightly on the lips. "I'll be back tomorrow, Jessi," he said softly. "I hope you'll be waiting for me."

Eleven

Kale returned the next afternoon while Amanda was in school and Jessi had run home to start a dinner she hoped to serve to the three of them that night. She heard him on the porch. Before she could greet him at the door, the screen was slamming and she was swept into his arms, his mouth was fastened to hers, his tongue probing and stroking in her mouth.

He steered her into the guest room where he slowly undressed her, then shed his own clothes and covered her with kisses from her face to her thighs, stopping only to probe and excite and send her bucking out of control on the sheets.

Then he lowered himself gently upon her, cradled between her legs and made love to her with infinite care and passion, driving her over the edge again and again until she felt boneless. Then she held him close while he tensed and collapsed. Exhausted, he rolled alongside her and pulled her against him, edging lower so that his mouth was against her breast.

In all the time that passed since he entered the door, they

had not spoken a word. Now they lay entwined and he languidly flicked his tongue around her nipple.

She closed her eyes, grinned at the ceiling and fought an urge to give in when she began to feel the faint stirring of desire Kale was once again inciting with his tongue. He was an impossible man who made love insatiably and gently, and she was shocked at her own behavior when she reacted to him.

She hadn't known how it could be. She hadn't known until he showed her.

"Why did you bring me in here?" she asked him.

"Have you ever made love in here before?"

"No."

"Good. I hoped not," he told her softly, sucking on her nipple.

"Kale, we have some things to talk about," she reminded, smiling at the top of his black hair.

"Yes," he agreed, and with a kiss on her breast, pulled away from her and rested his head on his hand, his elbow balanced on the bed.

"I thought, that is, before the Burness accident and afterward, I thought we were...close. At least, wanting each other. And then, when you came back yesterday, you were so... distant," she told him. "And now—"

He inhaled deeply as though girding himself to tackle an unpleasant problem. "I thought you had played me for a fool again," he said. "I don't know how I feel about you, Jessi, I just know I want you."

She stared at him, disappointed, feeling curiously rejected and vulnerable, for she was beginning to suspect what she was feeling for him went far beyond wanting.

His eyes were on her breasts. He leaned over to kiss her gently and flick his tongue over a nipple, and then he said, "I had a dream that first night I was in the hospital, a terrible wonderful dream, and you were a part of it. Only I thought it was real, that my world had evolved differently over the last twelve years. I can't seem to shake its effects." He searched her face for understanding. "Have you ever had a revelation and knew afterward that you would never again be the same? That, somehow, everything would look different after... I'm not making sense, am I? It was a crazy dream. And so real it sent me into hell for a few days."

"Tell me about it," she whispered, brushing a strand of straight black hair off his forehead. She wanted to know.

"I wish I could. Maybe someday."

"Do you know, I'm not sure I understand about revelations changing one's life, but since you've come back into mine, nothing has been the same."

He grinned lazily at her and let his thumb wander from her breast up her chest and neck. "Ditto," he muttered. "You have a way about you, Jessi Caldwell, that draws me in time after time."

Slowly he pulled her toward him, removed his thumb and pressed his mouth over hers. His hand slid down her bare back and pulled her backside so that the fronts of their bodies were pressed close.

Jessi pushed on his chest to separate them. "Amanda is due home from school soon," she warned.

"Tonight then?"

"I had planned to fix dinner and have you join us. That's why I was at home in the middle of the afternoon. The perks of being the owner," she told him, sliding from the bed.

When she pulled her clothes in front of her, he stilled her hands. "You're beautiful, Jessi," he said softly. "Don't hide from me."

"I'm not beautiful, Kale," she told him.

"Then you don't know. You've always been beautiful, and now, well, now you're even more so, now that I've seen all of you," he said, pulling the clothes away and looking at her. "I've never seen a woman's body that was more beautiful than yours."

She could see that the admiration in his eyes was real and she was speechless with awe. She could also see what his gaze was stirring up, and so she sidestepped and fled to her room to dress. It was like the old days, when she felt beautiful with the boy next door. Don't think about that, she warned herself. That had been pure, innocent love.

While she prepared dinner, she sang. She put two whole fryers on the enclosed barbecue, stirred together her favorite potato dish and mixed a vegetable salad. By then Amanda was home.

"Cloth napkins?"

"Yes, cloth napkins."

"We only use cloth napkins for special occasions."

"Well, people like Kale Noble expect cloth napkins."

"We never made a fuss about him before, not when he was staying here," Amanda observed suspiciously. "You hardly ever even came home, and you *never* cooked."

"We're welcoming him this time. He's going to be staying a whole week."

"But not here." Amanda pouted. "I don't see why you couldn't let him stay here."

"He made his own reservations, Amanda. I'm sure he doesn't want to impose. Last time there wasn't room anywhere and he *had* to stay here," Jessi reminded.

"I still don't know why you're making such a fuss. I mean, I really like Kale, but you never used to hardly talk to him."

"We've become pretty close," she said.

Amanda bobbed her eyebrows in understanding. "Oh yeah?"

When Kale came in for dinner, he sought out Jessi and zeroed in on her, scooping her into his arms and hugging her soundly. "Amanda's going to feel slighted," she whispered in his ear.

He also hugged Amanda generously. "How's your computer class?" he asked.

"I'm learning zillions of things, and I can beat Jaime Ho-ganson at Solar Combat," she said when her feet were solidly on the floor. "I think I might like to be a civil engineer when I grow up," she added slyly.

"Ah, a *civil* engineer," he acknowledged with a half grin.

"I know that's what you are. I asked my computer teacher. She told me about the, uh, Computer Assisted Design system you use. She said it's three dimensional," Amanda said eagerly. "You call it CAD."

"Very good," he said. "We call it CAD. I use it all the time. Maybe some time you'd like to come to Minneapolis and see our office and labs."

"Could I? Could I really?"

"I'll arrange it," he said.

Jessi listened to their conversation with small fingers of fear crawling over the back of her neck. If she hadn't been so euphoric that he was back, that he was staying for a week, that he seemed to be enthralled with her, she might have given more thought to his words. Amanda in Minneapolis? With Kale? Or with her grandparents? Visiting, or living?

As it was, Jessi pushed the niggling fears and questions from her mind and enjoyed the meal with Kale and Amanda. Kale appeared to be surprised at the quality of the dinner, and she chided him for expecting less from her. After dinner, she reluctantly left them to relieve Chaz at the base, and when she returned they were deep into solving a problem using Kale's laptop.

At dusk the three of them swam, then Kale returned to his motel room and Jessi and Amanda showered and watched television. It was nearly midnight, long after Amanda was in bed, that Kale found Jessi in the gazebo, where they'd agreed to meet.

She was watching the moon rise over the lake from behind the fine screen that kept out mosquitoes, hoping he would appear. She had lit one of the brass torches, and he had found her. She knew what he wanted.

It was what she wanted, too.

He kissed her thoroughly and unbuttoned her blouse. "I've

been waiting hours for you," he whispered. "I don't want to take it slow."

She flicked off the torch. "Neither do I."

He complied, stripping off her clothes while she frantically yanked at his until they were naked on the double air mattress, connected eagerly in writhing, penetrating rapture.

And then, much later, he took her slowly, languidly, completely, and with a tenderness that left tears in her eyes.

Neither of them wanted to part, and the parting took a long time. By the time Jessi returned to the cabin and crawled into her bed it was nearly dawn.

Chaz did not question her the next morning, although he looked at her quizzically, as though he knew where she had been and what she had been doing.

"Kale is using our rental car all week," she told him. "But if we need it for customers, I'll just let him take mine."

Chaz nodded, eyeing her warily, his lips pursed. "I see," he said, and Jessi suspected that for once he saw entirely too much.

"Is Pelly working on Carlson's tail dragger today?" she asked, sorting through the mechanic's schedule.

"Uh-huh," he said, still studying her suspiciously.

"Did the part for the Skyhawk come in?"

"Uh-huh."

"And did we get the new logbooks yet?"

"Uh-uh. Jessi?"

"Hmm?"

"What in hell is Noble doing here for a whole week?"

"Well, I'm not sure. I don't know much about what he does when he's at the bridge site," she replied.

"They don't work on weekends since they finished pouring the supports. What's he going to do here over two whole days of weekend?"

She replied with a frown.

"Okay, okay," he relented with frustration, throwing both

of his arms up with characteristic melodrama. "I'll pretend you weren't Rollie's wife all those years."

She regarded him solemnly, ignoring his goading. "Are you taking the Gulbran's charter this afternoon?"

"Yes," he barked and slammed the screen door as he left. She saw him through the window with his fists stuffed deeply into his pants pockets, stomping toward the mechanics' shed. By nightfall, everyone in Kenross would know Jessi Morris was having an affair with that dark, handsome engineer who designed the Point Six bridge.

It didn't seem to matter what people said, for she was insulated from the gossip. Rarely did anyone see them together that week, except Amanda. He spent most of his days at the bridge because Curt Burness had asked him to; his early evenings were spent with Jessi and Amanda, and later, Kale and Jessi wound their way to the isolated gazebo and made love until the early hours of the morning.

Often, he found his way back to her house when Amanda was at her computer class, and he made love to her in the afternoon in the guest bedroom.

Never did she see the inside of his motel room. Never did he set foot in her bedroom. During that week, he didn't show his face at the airfield, except on Sunday when Jessi flew him and Amanda for a picnic near the Canadian border.

Contrary to Chaz's observations, the bridge crew did work on Saturday. Sunday was the only day of vacation Kale had.

She revelled in his voracious appetite for her, and she found herself counting the hours until they could be together. Sometimes they came together in a frenzy; sometimes it was gently and slowly. On Monday night, Kale simply held her while they watched the moon over the water and listened to the fish splash. It wasn't until early morning that they finally formed the night's perfect union.

And in spite of their frequent lovemaking, they talked for hours.

They talked about the identical swing sets in their back-

yards, favorite meeting spots for the Caldwell girls and the
Noble boys, the bridge games that kept their parents up late
at least once a week, their traditional shared Christmas Eves
that were so special to both families. And then Kale revealed
his observation that the rift between the families had begun
occurring long before the accident, when Charlotte had flung
herself at Paul, taunting and teasing, daring him to fall for her.

Jessi hadn't seen that, and when the tension stirred between
them, they changed the topic, as if neither of them wanted to
bring past unpleasantness into their lives, as if they were starting over, or more accurately, in Jessi's painful opinion, as if
they were both in a bubble and reality was locked outside.

After that, they talked about impersonal things, Kale's work,
how he felt about his designs, how he ran his business, how
it had grown, the plans he had for the future, the intriguing
new proposal he was bidding on in Louisiana. They spoke of
Jessi's work, how she loved flying, what she saw in the future
for her aviation business, the planes she wanted to buy and
fly, the places she wanted to see.

Not once did they speak of his parents and whether he had
spoken to them about Amanda being their granddaughter. She
wanted to ask, but she didn't want to interrupt the magic.

As the days and nights passed, she caught him more and
more often simply studying her, or touching her face or
smoothing back her unruly curls, his endearments falling off
after the first few nights. He no longer told her she was beautiful, but he looked at her for long moments, and ran his hands
over her body frequently.

He no longer told her what he thought of their lovemaking,
or how she made him feel, but he clutched her tightly to him
for a long time after they were both satisfied, and he lingered
often over her lips, tasting her, nibbling, giving her a part of
himself that was tender and loving.

Sometimes he held her as though he would never let her
go, as though he was absorbing her under his skin and taking
her into his heart.

Was this only physical lovemaking?

She wasn't sure. She was afraid to think ahead. When the week was up, he would be gone. She didn't want to think about that either, what it would be like after he was gone. Even if he cared for her, she couldn't have him. His future included children, and she was never going to have a child.

And then it was Thursday night, and he was leaving the next day. They sat together in the wicker settee, their feet on the coffee table. She was tucked under his arm as they sat in silence, listening to a light rain on the gazebo roof. They had dressed partially after making love. He wore his khaki shorts and she wore shorts, her sleeveless blouse unbuttoned over her lacy bra. Their shoes were scattered alongside the air mattress.

His fingers played an absent tattoo on her bare shoulder, and her left hand lay flat on his right thigh.

"It's time that Amanda met her grandparents," he said softly.

She found her hand gripping his thigh at the shock of his words. A wild hysteria burst somewhere in her midsection, spreading like poison.

"Jessi? We talked of this before," he said, obviously sensing that she was disturbed.

"Why now?"

"What does that mean?"

"You've waited until your last night here. Why haven't we talked about this before?" she cried, accusing.

"You didn't ask. I waited for you to ask," he said quietly.

"I shouldn't have to ask. It's your call. I didn't want to press you for answers, or about timing. I didn't know you were going to spring this on me our last night together."

"Why does it have to be something divisive between us?" he questioned.

"You know it is. You waited until the last night to bring it up," she said, remembering suddenly how he had invited Amanda to visit his business on the first night of his stay. He hadn't asked or given Jessi a chance to agree. He had simply announced.

She pulled away from him and sat on the edge of the settee. "You planned this all week. You knew when you came here you were going to do this, didn't you? You invited Amanda to visit you in Minneapolis."

"Jessi," he pleaded softly, reaching for her. "You sound as if I'm fighting you on this."

She jerked away from his touch and stood, pacing away from him, around the back of the settee, coming around to his side. "A week of free sex, and now it's over, you're down to business, aren't you?" The words erupted, sounding brutal, but reflecting the fear and pain she had dreaded all week.

"Is that what you think?"

"Of course, it's what I think. The sex has been good. Now it's over and the past is closed, too, isn't it?"

He flinched. "What do you mean?"

The words poured from her, forming somewhere she couldn't reach within herself, words bred of fear and anger and a long time of festering. "For old times' sake, to satisfy an old...lust. Isn't that what we both wanted? Coming together like this, to see what it would be like?" She inhaled sharply and more words poured out. "Now you want to take away the only member of my family I have left. Is revenge sweet?"

He was frowning, reaching for her, but she jerked away. "Stop it," he said. "I'm not trying to hurt you."

"You can't hurt me. I'd have to have feelings for you, wouldn't I, to be hurt? You can't hurt me again, Kale Noble," she charged.

"Again?"

"Surely you remember the last time, when you discovered what my parents had done and you blamed me." She pointed venomously at him. "I was sixteen. Sixteen! Blinded by a foolish puppy love. Just how aware do you think I was of what my parents were doing?" She circled him, not allowing him to speak. "I didn't find out Amanda was Paul's until after

Charlotte died. I didn't find out how she lied and my parents backed her up until I read the letter she left behind for me. I didn't know my father manipulated the witnesses to the accident. I didn't know they started rumors to break us up so that I would go back to Kenross and stay there and take care of Charlotte and their only grandchild. I hid Charlotte's pregnancy because I was so…ashamed of her. Ashamed! Sure, I had suspicions that things weren't quite right, and if I had been twenty-five, I'd probably have had the maturity to question them. But I wasn't, and I didn't. And you drove me away with your accusations because I didn't know what you were talking about. But when I saw the looks on all those faces watching us, I knew—I just *knew*—that everybody else had information I didn't have about my parents and what they had done. So I ran away, and when I was nineteen I married a man who loved me and trusted me and who was always there, and we were happy here. Until he died."

He waited for her to finish, studying her as if he hadn't really looked at her before.

"Why did you wait until now? When did you intend to tell her? When did you decide all this? Before last Wednesday, I imagine," she said angrily. "Why couldn't we have spent some time discussing it?"

He reached out and clasped her wrist. "Sit down, Jessi," he ordered softly. "I'm not trying to hurt you. Sit down and we can talk."

"We don't talk," she cried. "We've never had a meaningful discussion." That wasn't exactly true, she realized in retrospect. They had discussed many things, and in some depth, when they were teens and in the past week. But she continued anyway, as if she didn't remember that. "Just tell me what you plan to do. There isn't much I can do to stop you whether I like it or not," she told him, pulling against his hand, but not hard enough to break the contact.

He dropped her wrist and leaned forward, resting his elbows on his knees, clasping his hands. He was silent for a long time while she stood behind the settee and let hot tears roll down her cheeks.

"I think we should tell her who her father was tomorrow morning."

There was a hard note creeping into his voice. It was the voice she had come to recognize as uniquely his, and she had not heard it for weeks. She realized as he spoke that she had not heard his anger or felt the sting of his restless energy all week.

"Then what?" she demanded.

"Then we'll play it by ear. Give her time to adjust."

"How long?"

"Dammit, Jessi," he retorted. "We have a right to know her. Let's tell her the truth and leave it up to her, okay?"

What had she done? Had her apprehension about this moment created the panic that colored her words? The bittersweet expectation of ended bliss had driven her into a kind of hysteria she couldn't control. It was over. She had known it would end.

She hadn't expected it to hurt so much.

She wiped away the tears and cleared her throat. "She's like my own child," she said. "I'll never have a child of my own, and I've had her since she was a baby. I just can't imagine what it will be like to have her taken away."

She reached to touch his shoulder, but found him rigid and unresponsive. He was shutting her out. He was letting her know he was done with her. He said he wanted to discuss the situation, but she didn't believe him.

She thought he simply wanted to dictate terms and get it done with now that he had satisfied his "wanting" her.

He stood, digging his hands into his pockets. She could see in the dim light that his pose was deceptively relaxed. He was angry. She felt the energy radiating ominously from him. And when he spoke, she believed she had been right to have suspicions about his motives, for it was the old Kale with the biting words.

"We agreed some time ago that we would tell her the truth. We agreed that the Nobles have a right to know her. I've kept to my part of our bargain, and I know my parents will want to meet her. I haven't told them yet." He moved toward the rug and slipped into his shoes. "Contrary to your suspicions, my dear, I did not have this planned a week ago. I was waiting until I was healthy again before we faced this, and then, this week, other things took precedence, which may have been a foolish presumption on my part."

She watched him hunker to tie his shoes, and then stand to face her.

She felt him distancing himself from her, only it wasn't just a matter of him moving away, he was ripping a part of himself out of her, and it hurt with the agony of a fresh wound.

"I'll be by at nine," he said, moving to the door.

But the door didn't open. He stood there in silence, and finally, his low voice broke through the stillness. "Was Rollie in the picture back then? Was that part true?"

She knew it must have cost him to ask that, but her hurt and anger were at a peak, and her response flew into the darkness before she had time to think. "I married him, didn't I? What do *you* think?"

Her caustic words were met with yet another silence. Then she heard the gazebo screen door squeak open, squeak shut.

She felt a wild, illogical urge to call him back. If they parted on angry words, they were finished.

They were finished anyway.

Let him go, she advised herself. She was better off without the turbulence he wrought in her life.

"I didn't know that what we had was so frail," he said, his voice coming like a disembodied spirit from beyond the screen. "I don't want to be blindsided a second time." He sounded weary. "I'll see you in the morning, Jessi, and we'll break the news to Amanda as gently as we can."

Twelve

Kale sat in his motel room and wished he had stopped to buy a bottle of brandy. He wanted a drink. He wanted to feel the stinging sharp heat of good liquor burning his throat and warming his insides.

The mid-August evening was warm and humid, but his skin was clammy and his insides were cold and aching. He could smell her on his skin. He could smell the erotic aroma of sweat and sex blended with the faint residue of Jessi's unique scent. He could feel her soft and slick, taking him to places he had never been before.

She had captivated him, hypnotized him, blinded him to all but what he had begun to crave from her. She had seeped into his very pores, settled into his heart, blanketed his mind so that he thought only of her, waited to be with her, wanted her so deeply he thought he would burst before they finally came together late in the night.

He had dreaded leaving her at the end of the week, tried to conjure up reasons for her to come with him and made excuses to stay near the bridge site when, in truth, there had been little for him to do at Point Six during the last few days. He simply hadn't wanted to fly away from her, not knowing how she felt, wondering what she had done to him that he found himself in such a state.

He could never have guessed she would overshadow every other woman he had ever been with. He had spent twelve years resenting and blaming her.

And then there had been the accident at the construction site, and the baffling dream that altered everything. He had awakened from it to find, once more, that she had not kept her promise to see him before she left. It had seemed such a small thing to ask, but it was significant to him for reasons he hadn't yet admitted.

The next day, after his release from the hospital, he had been torn between angry disappointment and wondering if she had come back to him while he was sleeping. Had she come back?

For over two weeks he had squashed thoughts of Jessi when they appeared, but could think of little else. He had assigned Mike to handle the Point Six bridge monitoring, intending it to be permanent. It took just a little over two weeks, but finally he gave in.

He was lost after that.

Once she was in his arms, once he felt her mouth under his, his blood had raced out of control, and he remembered the part of the dream when he had been happy and none of the bad things in his life had ever had a chance to happen.

He remembered in the dream that they had been together forever, and he had needed her and trusted her, and suddenly, holding her in his arms behind the counter of her office, there had been only one thing that mattered. It was loving her and knowing she loved him back, as it should have been between them over the last twelve years.

For the last week, day and night, Jessi had been his focus, his need, his very life.

He waited for a cue from her to discuss Amanda. He wanted to tell her how he looked forward to introducing his parents to Amanda.

Only today had he begun to pull himself back to reality, that other reality, where decisions were painful and people could not be trusted and his gut churned with the fear that he had fallen under her spell again and there would be a terrible consequence to pay. As there had been before.

The bliss of the past week had fallen away like a discarded garment when he and Jessi finally did speak of Amanda. He had wanted to bring it up before, but he also wanted to give Jessi time to adjust to sharing the child she considered a daughter.

He discovered during their last hour together that it might have been a mistake to delay introducing the sensitive issue that loomed between them. Then again, discussing it sooner might have served only to interrupt their passionate sojourn.

When finally he couldn't put it off any longer, she pulled away from him, accused him, belittled what he had thought was the beginning of something beautiful they had been cheated of earlier in their lives.

It had cut mortally, and yet, he felt as though he had been waiting for it, expecting it, dreading it. He knew, had known since the issue first came up, that Jessi would not give up Amanda.

That was the real world.

Fate had played her false, preventing her from having children of her own. Still, there were his parents to consider.

And himself.

Jessi had lost more than any one person should have to bear, he thought, remembering how she had finally explained that they had both been manipulated by her parents back then.

She wouldn't admit she had been faithful to him. But he knew. The Jessi he knew had not been unfaithful.

It was small solace, however, when he was slammed with

the realization she neither loved him nor trusted him, but was concerned only with keeping Amanda to herself.

It was painfully clear to him that the past week had been an illusion of happiness.

She had never intended to share Amanda with the Nobles. She had apparently hoped to distract him and to manipulate him so that he would fail to follow through in bringing Amanda together with her grandparents.

He loathed himself that she continued to beguile him like a siren angel even while he saw her flaws.

Damn the dream that had seemed to turn back the hands of time. Damn her unnatural power over him. Damn her sexy body. And his own self-destructive needs.

It was a torturous night, and a grim morning. He called Phil to bring the plane to Kenross for his return trip. He drove Jessi's rental car to the base and had Chaz take care of the lease forms. He left his cases and suit jacket, tie folded neatly in the pocket, in the office.

Then he walked to Jessi's house, arriving promptly at nine o'clock. He knocked on the door and entered when he saw her through the screen door standing several feet from him with a dish towel in her hands. He hated himself for wanting to sweep her into his arms and pretend she had not accused him.

He watched her searching his face, and he held himself absolutely still, showing nothing of himself but the deliberately immutable wall that protected him.

Then he saw Amanda, looking to him for answers, seeking something tangible with wide-eyed innocence. He knew when he saw her face that Jessi had talked to her, warned her of something. He hoped Jessi had not caused damage he would be unable to undo.

Amanda threw herself against him, and he held her close, letting the fleeting thought pass quickly that someday he might have a daughter like this, and what would he want for her?

Certainly not a wounded heart. What would he say to her if she were his own daughter?

He looked up at Jessi, who looked as miserable as he felt. "Well?"

Her focus was on the girl who trembled against him. "We have to talk, honey," she said gently.

He led Amanda to the dining room table and sat down around the corner from her. Jessi followed behind him and sat on the other side of Amanda. He looked to Jessi to explain what had been said between them this morning. Jessi understood.

"I've told Amanda that we have something very important to say to her, something that will be a shock, and...well, we were just waiting for you to get here to tell her."

He avoided Jessi's eyes. He saw too much in them, remembered too much, felt too much he no longer wanted to feel.

He took Amanda's hands in his, and when he felt how cold they were, he rubbed them. If she were his daughter...

He spoke from the heart, keeping his voice soft and gentle as he spoke. "I hope you know I care deeply for you, Amanda, and I don't want to hurt you. But I'm afraid what we have to tell you may hurt you a great deal, and confuse you, too. And it may even make you angry. I'm going to start a long time ago, before you were born, when your mother was in love with a young man named Paul. They made a very handsome couple. They loved each other very much, and they wanted to get married."

He watched Amanda's eyes widen and her teeth capture her lower lip. She looked terribly afraid.

"One night, they were together in a car and they had an accident. A very bad accident. Paul was killed."

"Killed?" she asked, her voice so small and frightened, he squeezed her hands tighter in reassurance.

"Your mother married another man, but now comes the complicated part, Amanda. Your mother and Paul...well, your mother was pregnant. She was going to have a baby, and Paul was the father. She accepted the proposal of Frank Morris, a man she had known, a man who also loved her, a man she obviously cared about, and she married him. Her baby, the baby she and Paul made, grew up believing Frank Morris was her real father.''

He stopped when her face whitened and her mouth opened in a silent scream. His eyes instinctively went to Jessi, as did Amanda's.

"He's right, honey," Jessi soothed as she rose and kneeled alongside the girl's chair. Amanda threw herself into Jessi's arms, and then slid off the chair and the two clutched each other kneeling on the floor.

Kale sat very still, his hands clasped together on the table, and he watched them.

"My daddy! He *was* my dad! You can't take him away from me again!" Amanda cried. "He died but he's still my dad!''

"Of course he was, Amanda," Jessi purred. "Of course. He was your dad in every way and he loved you more than he loved anyone else on earth. He'll always be your dad, and nobody wants you to deny him. That isn't what Kale wants at all.''

"My daddy!" she cried, and Kale realized for the first time that Frank Morris had likely been a good father, a kind and loving and attentive father, and she had lost him. The girl was probably still grieving. Could he have handled this more sensitively? He wondered if he might have handled it with more gentleness.

"You had two fathers, Amanda," Jessi was saying. "You had two fathers. I know it sounds kind of mixed up. It's like you almost had two mothers, too, you know. I love you as though you are my own daughter. You know that, don't you? And you love me, too. And you loved your real mother, just as she loved you, too. It's never made you seem disloyal, has it? Nobody has ever asked you to stop loving one of us, have they?''

Amanda shook her head a little wildly, her curls falling over her tear-stained face as Jessi held her away from her.

"Well, now you have had two fathers, too, and you don't have to choose between loving them, even though they're both gone."

For a moment, Kale's suspicious mind harbored the thought that she was going to turn Amanda against Paul and the Nobles.

He interjected, "Paul's mom and dad are your grandparents. Their names are Regina and Matthew. I know, when I tell them about you, they're going to be anxious to meet you—"

"When you're ready," Jessi finished. "They won't want to force themselves on you. Whenever you're ready, they'll want to meet you."

He heard her resisting him. Again his suspicions surfaced, and then he realized, whatever her motivation, what Jessi said was wise. Amanda would surely not respond if she thought she were being coerced.

"There's one other thing you should know," Jessi said, wiping Amanda's tears with a tissue. "Your father's last name."

"Noble," Kale said, his voice almost failing him.

Amanda turned to him in astonishment. "Noble? Like you?"

"Paul was my older brother," he said, his voice giving way. He cleared his throat but found he was still a little hoarse. "You're my niece, Amanda."

"Was he like you?" she asked weakly. "Was he dark and tall like you?"

"He was the handsome one," Kale replied. "His hair was sandy blond, kind of like Jessi's. And yours."

"I knew there was something special about you," she said, but her words ended in a dry sob. She turned her red eyes to Jessi and laid her head on Jessi's shoulder.

"How come nobody ever told me?" she asked.

If Jessi hadn't been accusatory and defensive last night, they might have discussed how to handle just that, he thought. It was one of the questions Amanda would inevitably ask, and the answer was condemning for Jessi and Charlotte, and, yes, even Frank Morris, who must have suspected the truth when Amanda was born only seven and a half months after their hasty wedding.

"I didn't know until after the plane crash," Jessi said. "Your mother left me a letter she had written several years ago explaining a lot of things about the accident that killed Paul Noble." Kale didn't miss the glance she aimed at him. "And then two months ago when Kale began coming to Kenross, well, after he met you he started to wonder, so we talked about it, and I told him the truth, and we decided to come and tell you together."

Amanda frowned at Kale. "You knew last month and only now you're telling me?"

Jessi put a gentle hand on her niece's forearm. "I think he wanted to get to know you first, and then he was rushed with the concrete pouring, and then we had the storm, and the accident, and now, finally—"

"You had all week," Amanda accused quietly.

He watched Jessi struggle with her answer. "I don't know why we put it off until today. I guess I just wanted to have you to myself for a little while longer. That was selfish of me," she admitted. Kale was impressed that she was honest about it.

"I think I'm really mad about this," Amanda said, sobbing again. "And I just want to cry and cry."

"Go ahead, Amanda. Go ahead and cry," Jessi said.

They sat in silence while the young girl cried in Jessi's arms. He avoided Jessi's eyes, and she probably avoided his. It seemed a long time, and finally the sobs lessened.

"Kale has to go to work, but I think he'd stay if you want him to," Jessi said softly, still holding Amanda in her arms.

Amanda looked up and turned toward him, her face swollen and red. "Will you come back again?"

"Yes, of course," he replied. "If you want me to."

"I do."

"I'd like to take you to see your grandparents, if you want to see them," he said.

"I...I don't know..." she blurted and wrinkled her face into more sobbing.

Jessi frowned at him. "We can talk about that later," she said. "We can decide later."

He could see that Jessi was hoping Amanda wouldn't want to see them. Might she go as far as discouraging Amanda from getting to know her grandparents just because she couldn't have children of her own?

The anger he felt toward Jessi was welcome, almost a relief, because it overwhelmed the wanting. He rose, then, and took a few steps so that he stood over the two females. He dropped to his haunches and touched Amanda. "I'll be back," he said. "Here's my card. You can call me anytime. Collect. Day or night. Anytime." He laid it on the table and rose.

He stood for a few moments, wishing Amanda would turn to him, let him hold her before he left. But she was clinging to Jessi, whose eyes were pressed shut.

He zeroed in on Jessi and she opened her eyes. Like a silent telegram her gaze confirmed the end of their intimacy. He wasn't sure how long they stared at each other, and later, he couldn't describe what had been in her eyes that had been so painfully lucid, but the communication passed between them as if it had been shouted.

Silently he walked away from them, letting himself out.

Phil was waiting at the airfield, talking to Chaz while he fueled the plane. Kale nodded perfunctorily to Chaz, entered the passenger side and buckled himself in, noting that his suit jacket lay neatly over the back of the seat. He opened his briefcase, hoping he might wipe the last half hour's scene from his mind if he worked on the Louisiana project.

He was aware of Phil greeting him and slipping into the

seat next to him. "Good day for flying," he said to Kale, who nodded.

"Nice to see you again, Phil," he replied.

He saw Phil's hand reach for the controls when Chaz burst from the office, waving both hands above his head. "Wait," he said to Phil, who hadn't noticed the wild gesturing.

Phil opened his door.

"Hold it! Wait a minute!" Chaz shouted.

Phil shrugged and Kale looked at him, perplexed. Chaz returned to the office, and they waited, staring at each other. He opened his mouth to tell Phil to rev up, when he saw her.

It was Amanda flying across the parking lot, pushing through the gate, running down the sidewalk and onto the apron, careening around the wing on the passenger side. Kale wasted no time. His belt was unbuckled and he was out the door and on the ground when she slammed into him, knocking him backward into the fuselage.

"Whoa, whoa," Kale cautioned, laughing, lifting her up and holding her against his chest.

Her arms twined tightly around his neck. She kissed him on the cheek and the forehead. "I'm glad you're my uncle, Kale," she said between heaving breaths. "You tell my grandparents I do want to see them someday. And you come back soon, will you? I'm glad I know the truth. You will come back, won't you, Kale?"

"I'll come back, Amanda," he said. "You call me when you want me to come back. My work on the bridge is going to last for a few more months, but I won't be coming up here as often. I'll come up just to see you, though."

He hung onto her until she finally let loose of his neck and he could breathe freely again. He let her down until her feet hit the ground.

"Have a good flight," she said and looked up at the sky and especially to the west. "It's a good day. No weather in sight."

A budding pilot, he thought, like Jessi, loving the sky and

airplanes. He watched her face, the distinct Noble hairline and the dimples in her cheeks so like Jessi's. And the sandy hair, slightly frizzed around her face. She could be their daughter, his and Jessi's.

The thought unnerved him, left him feeling raw. It had been part of an old dream, being the father of Jessi's children.

But it could never happen.

She saluted Phil and watched them from the sidewalk until they taxied out of sight. When Phil revved up at the end of the runway, Kale heard Amanda's young voice clear and mischievously businesslike on the radio. "Five niner November cleared for takeoff."

Kale, mindful of his own amusement, saw Phil grinning. Under her quiet exterior, the kid was a fireball.

Just like Jessi.

Thirteen

Oversleeping had never been a problem for Jessi, but when the telephone rang it was nine-thirty.

Still stuporous from heavy sleep, she found it difficult to concentrate on Kale's earnest words flowing from the telephone.

"My mother wants to take my father up to meet Amanda," he said with some urgency, perhaps for the third time. She was slowly reaching awareness.

"What?"

"Jessi, are you all right?" he asked finally.

"I, I think so. Who…oh, yes, your parents. How are they?"

"They've never been better, actually," he replied with a hint of impatience. "I told them yesterday about Amanda, and my father…my father…smiled. For a few seconds he looked like he used to look in the old days when Paul was alive. My mother wants to take him to visit Amanda. Now. Today."

She heard the vague questioning in his voice, and she hesitated, wondering whether Amanda would be receptive, wondering if it might be too soon to have them visit, wondering whether Matthew Noble might emerge from his self-imposed prison if he saw Paul's daughter, wondering what Kale expected her to say, wondering if he had thought about what they had experienced with each other during the last week.

"Jessi, what's the matter with you?"

"I was sleeping. I can't believe I was still sleeping." She cleared her throat and sat up in bed. "Okay, I think I'm conscious now. What do you want me to do?"

He gave a short laugh. "Damned if I know. This seems to be out of our hands at this point. I hope you won't deny them."

"Of course not." She was almost insulted that he would think she would be cruel to his parents, who had been her *other* mom and dad all her life until Paul's accident. "But I won't guarantee what Amanda's reaction will be. She hasn't had much time to adjust to all this." She hoped he took it as a warning and not a threat.

"I did try to discourage my mother with just that line, but she's willing to take the risk. My father hasn't responded to *anything* in over a decade. This is the first time— I can't bring myself to stop them."

"I'll handle it somehow," she told him, dangling her feet over the edge of the bed, studying the clock. Her eyes weren't deceiving her. "It will be nice to see your parents again."

"It's the first time my mother has been excited about anything since before Paul's accident."

"Then I hope for their sake that Amanda is ready to see them. I'll talk to her."

"I have a meeting that's critical to the future of my business this afternoon," he said. "People are coming from Louisiana and I must be here."

"We'll try to see that they're comfortable," she assured, hoping Amanda was up to the emotional pressure of meeting grandparents she hadn't known about until last week.

"Jessi..." he started. "If anything goes wrong. I mean, if *anything* goes wrong, call me."

"I'll handle it, Kale," she told him. "Don't worry. I was always fond of your parents, and I haven't changed my attitude about them. They won't be thrown to the wolves. Trust me."

She heard a short laugh. "I'll try," he quipped. She could hear the smile. She could share the humor of the situation with him, although she said nothing. After all they had been through, the feuding, the perceived betrayals, the secrets, the lies that surrounded them, asking him to trust her seemed non-sensical.

They ended the conversation on an up note, and within half an hour Jessi was telling Amanda the news. "They're so anxious to meet you, they can't wait another day," she said, explaining the precarious state of Matthew Noble's mental health, and hoping Amanda was up to coping with the impending event.

Amanda was stunned, then angry, then curious, then anxious. And, finally, oddly pensive.

When the familiar Noble Engineering aircraft finally landed, Jessi was in her office on the telephone, Chaz was in the mechanics' shed and Amanda, who was gassing a plane, didn't notice it.

Neither did Jessi until it was already taxiing toward her. She ended her conversation as gracefully as possible and flew down the steps to warn Amanda, who was standing on the stepladder leaning over a high wing fueling the tank.

She was finishing her job, replacing the cap and making her way down the ladder to replace the hose when she looked up and saw the familiar plane coming close, prop spinning, blowing her hair back.

Jessi stood on the sidewalk staring at her niece, who was frozen in place with the gas hose in her hand.

When the Bonanza props abruptly jerked to a stop, Amanda wandered in dazed awe toward the front of the plane, stopping suddenly when she reached the length of the gas hose. She simply stood, mesmerized, as she watched Phil emerge, walk around the plane, and open the passenger door.

Phil extended a hand to a white-haired man, slightly stooped and thin. He wore a short-sleeve white shirt and khaki pants. Matthew Noble was barely recognizable, a shadow of the dynamic, athletic father she remembered who used to toss a football with his oldest son on the front lawn, and successfully managed his own engineering firm when Jessi was a child.

Jessi watched, moving forward warily, as Kale's father shuffled slowly toward his granddaughter, who continued holding the gas hose, now precariously pointed at him. Jessi slipped behind Amanda, smiled at the narrowly focused, staring eyes of Matthew's aged face, and forced the nozzle out of her niece's fist.

"Amanda," she said softly. "Meet Matthew Noble, your grandfather. Matthew, meet Paul's daughter, Amanda."

"She looks like Jessi," Matthew croaked. "And she looks like Paul. Same jaw line. Same color hair." Then he held out a hand and touched her forearm. "So you're Paul's girl."

"Y-you don't look at all...like K-Kale," Amanda stammered.

Jessi set the gas nozzle in place and turned when she heard a cry from the plane, and there was Regina Noble as lovely as always, in spite of a faceful of fine wrinkles. Her silvery hair complimented her olive skin. "Oh, Jessi," she cried, standing by the wing of the plane, her long, elegant fingers forming a steeple under her chin while she waited for, what? Jessi's response? Amanda's affection? Feared rejection?

Jessi felt an uncommon warmth encase her, and the years disappeared. Mrs. Noble had been more than the *other* mom when Jessi was a girl. Mrs. Noble had been the mom she might have chosen if babies had choice and wisdom. How could she have kept that feeling buried all these years, she wondered, as she strode quickly to share an embrace with the woman she had loved and taken for granted as a child?

"Reggie Mom," she cried as she embraced the frail body

that still smelled like sweet roses. "Reggie Mom," she murmured again. She had grown up calling Regina Noble Reggie
Mom, and now the name and the old feelings slipped into the
present from wherever they had been concealed all these years.

"Little Jessi," Regina sighed, holding her tightly. "You
look wonderful. How glorious it is to see you again, all grown
up and beautiful."

She laughed at the kind description, assailed by an overflow
of memories, which included Regina's gentle and persistent
affection for Little Jessi, the smile that lit up her face whenever
Jessi burst through the kitchen door of the Noble house. "Jessi
Caldwell! You crawled under the hole in the hedge again!"
she would scold and brush the tell-tale sand from the front of
Jessi's shirt, laughing and shaking her head. "However are we
going to turn you into a lady when the time comes?"

Regina must have been thinking of the same thing. "We
didn't need to worry so about you growing up, did we, dear?
You've turned out beautifully."

"I still crawl through holes if I have to." Jessi laughed.

Regina held her at arms' length. "Well, I'm sure you do it
gracefully," she quipped, smiling, glancing for a second at the
front of Jessi's blouse. The affection in her eyes was unmistakable.

The old feelings had never died, Jessi realized, enjoying the
warm, comfortable softness of being in Mrs. Noble's company
again. She was assailed by memories of the spicy clean smells
of the Noble kitchen, and the vaguely mellow music always
in the background. And Reggie Mom always looking like the
mom in the ads, her thick black hair brushed off her face, her
eyes sparkling, her hands clean and nails polished, her blouse
tucked neatly into the belt of her perfectly fitted pants, emphasizing her trim figure.

But when Mrs. Noble's eyes darted toward her husband, her
eyes widened in an anticipation so heartfelt, it was almost
alarming, and she sucked in her lips as she observed, obvi-

ously as anxious to see the outcome as she was to participate in meeting her granddaughter.

Amanda and Matthew Noble seemed to be in a guarded conversation, neither of them relaxed or comfortable, but both of them intent on the other.

That, Jessi thought, as she and Regina slipped their hands behind each other's backs, was apparently a breakthrough for Kale's father.

As the pair moved gradually closer, Jessi heard Amanda say, "I never met my father. I didn't know he was my father until very recently. I already had a dad." Then her eyes flew to Jessi and Mrs. Noble. "There's Kale's mother. I can tell she's Kale's mother."

"Your grandmother, dear," Mrs. Noble said gently, smiling.

"She's Paul's little girl," Matthew Noble mused. "Paul's little girl." His eyes narrowed and scanned the horizon just above the trees around the parking lot, seeking. "Your little girl's here. Paul...we have your little girl." His words faded until only his mouth seemed to mime them.

Regina laid a hand softly on his shoulder and pressed her eyes closed. When she reopened them a moment later, she stepped toward Amanda, careful not to crowd the little girl, although she undoubtedly wanted to take her granddaughter into her arms. She was being sensitive to Amanda's visibly confused feelings.

Jessi had no doubt Regina would tread lightly around Amanda until the girl gave her some indication she would be invited closer.

"Amanda," Jessi said softly. "This is the woman I used to call Reggie Mom when I was a girl."

"Did my mom call her that, too?" Amanda asked, clinging to Jessi.

"No, dear, your mother always called me Mrs. Noble," Regina said, smiling a little sadly. "Your mother and I weren't as close as Jessi and I were. You look more like Jessi than your mother.''

Amanda grinned, relaxing slightly. ''I know. That's what everyone says. The genes got all mixed up, I guess.''

Regina laughed lightly and shook her head. ''Imagine talking about genes when you're twelve years old. We never heard of genes when we were young, and I'm not sure yet that I understand them exactly.''

''You look a little like Paul, too,'' Jessi added softly to Amanda.

''Yes,'' Regina agreed, studying her granddaughter. ''The hairline and around the lower part of your face. Kale has that hairline, too. Do you know, I think you could easily be mistaken for Jessi and Kale's daughter if one judged solely on looks.''

Jessi and Regina pulled away from each other then as Amanda stepped closer to her grandmother, and Jessi found herself nursing a shortness of breath when a sweet heat gripped her insides.

She and Kale producing a child who looked a little like both of them? Another painful fantasy.

She would never know what made her turn suddenly to search out Kale, who wasn't supposed to be there.

But she did turn on an inexplicable impulse, and Kale was standing there within earshot, standing alone alongside the still prop of his glossy white plane, standing frozen like a sculpture, except for the urgent flames sparkling in his intense, dark eyes.

Jessi was overwhelmed with the hopelessness of the thrill that had taken her breath away. Their eyes met, and held, across the short expanse of tarmac, while the rare and profound drama they had instigated was unfolding before them.

There was no doubt the occasion at the airfield would change all their lives.

Ironic, Jessi thought, that the changes were probably as trau-

matic as those foisted upon them by the tragic car accident
thirteen years ago, but these changes were reversing the hurts
and hates incited by the consequences of Charlotte's reckless
driving.

Jessi kept to herself the sickening fear that she was losing
Amanda, and the increasingly painful aftermath of her week-
long sojourn of lovemaking with Kale, now that their short
affair was over.

She put on the bright face the occasion called for and or-
chestrated their activities, checking weather for late afternoon
and finding it "iffy" for their return by plane to Minneapolis,
arranging for Kale and Phil to bunk in the two beds available
in the only vacant motel room nearby, scanning her cupboards
and freezer for a dinner meal, arranging beds for her other
guests.

Matthew and Regina needed separate rooms, and Amanda
had a couple of years ago discovered the gazebo was a frightening place to be at night when the wild forest sounds and
scents were her only company.

That left Jessi to sleep in the gazebo.

"I'll sleep there with you. We have two air mattresses,"
offered Amanda, wincing just a little.

Jessi grinned. "I don't mind sleeping there alone. In fact, I
rather like the idea," she told her niece, watching the relieved
smile on Amanda's face and avoiding the eyes of Kale who
was speaking to his mother by the fireplace.

He looked up momentarily, however, and she found herself
glancing askance. She girded herself against the electrifying
thought that he might think her words were an invitation to
join her again late in the night in the gazebo.

Surely, after their emotional finale, he would know that was
not her intent.

Did he still want her? Men, she thought, had a peculiar
ability to disassociate love and sex, and presumably Kale was
no exception. Still, she didn't want to believe the tenderness

with which he had made love to her didn't constitute something very special for both of them.

She knew it had been a once-in-a-lifetime experience for her.

Accept it, she warned herself, that for Kale it was an interlude, just the kind of old-fashioned dalliance men indulge in when opportunity arises, and he was now ready to move on, perhaps to find the woman who could give him a family.

Kale had probably had dozens of relationships. She, on the other hand, had had only an eight-and-a-half-year marriage to Rollie Morris, who had never introduced her to the bone-melting passion she had found with Kale.

It wasn't so easy for her to shake off the experience.

And now she also faced the imminent loss of Amanda.

"You have a most interesting home, Jessi," Regina observed, her conversation with Kale apparently finished. "Very appealing. I can see you and Amanda being very comfortable here." She glanced around at the ash panels and the stone fireplace. "Was it difficult for Amanda to leave her parents' home when they died?"

"She's had a room here since she was three years old," Jessi explained. "Charlotte was gone a lot of the time, and Amanda was in my care."

"Lucky Amanda," she murmured, and then added quickly, before Jessi could jump to Charlotte's defense, "the two of you seem to be so close. She's fortunate to have had two mother figures to turn to."

She smiled. "Like I did?"

"I hope you felt that way, my dear. You were like a daughter to me for so many years."

"What's with this family anyway?" Amanda puzzled. "Do we each get an extra set of parents? Like spares?"

Jessi and Regina joined in laughter. "Sometimes it seems like it," Jessi replied. "Reggie Mom was always there for me."

"And what about Grandma Caldwell?" Amanda questioned.

Jessi noted that the sudden tightness around Regina's mouth killed her smile.

Amanda was certainly aware there was little display of affection between Jessi and her parents, and she knew well that her own mother had resented their parents for what she called "smothering me." The Caldwell grandparents' summer visits had not been joyous occasions for either of the sisters.

Answering was a challenge that Jessi thought she might not be up to. She studied Amanda, seeing the defiance in her eyes, knowing her niece had conflicting feelings and thoughts. Hah, as if she didn't have a few inner conflicts of her own when it came to addressing the tensions between the Nobles and the Caldwells.

But Amanda, she recognized, might be the healing adhesive between the families. She thought of the Christmas Eves together, like they used to be.

"You know your grandmother Caldwell," she said. "What do you think it was like growing up with her?"

First, Amanda frowned in disappointment, and then she grinned strategically in understanding. Nodding, she briefly hugged Jessi's arm above the elbow.

Regina smiled. "I suppose it never hurts to have a backup parent around, does it?"

"Or grandparent," Jessi finished.

Regina and Amanda shared a warm breakthrough smile.

Breaking the comfortable silence, Kale announced, "The Burnesses have invited me to dinner. I'll be back late. See you in the morning." He squeezed his mother's hand and hugged Amanda against his side, avoiding contact with Jessi.

While Jessi watched, she wondered whether she should be offended that he had obviously postponed something as important as his Louisiana project in order to be here. Was it because he didn't trust her to treat his parents well?

When she caught his eye, she saw only smoldering blackness. What was he thinking, she wondered.

She thought about the gazebo where they had made love every night until dawn. She wanted to cry her eyes out when she saw him now, so close and so distant. So handsome, and unreadable.

He left then, and Amanda walked him to the restaurant where Curt Burness was planning to pick him up.

The three women prepared a light supper, and then Jessi excused herself so that Chaz could leave the airfield for the day. When she was closing up, she was called on a medical transport to Duluth with the victim of a grass fire.

While flying the chopper, she denied herself the expression of crying, but when the machine was tucked away for the night, she wept long and hard, sitting alone in the chopper's dark hangar until there were no more tears. Then she retreated to her cottage, where by now everyone was asleep. She showered and sat for a while on the front porch swing. The cottage was quiet and dark. It was after midnight.

She kicked off her shoes in the sand and walked silently onto the dock, realizing after several steps that someone was already there, sitting on the end. With the help of a three-quarter moon, she recognized Kale.

"What are you doing here?" she demanded in a hushed whisper.

"Probably the same thing you are," he replied.

She wasn't about to describe all the reasons she had for wanting to sit for a while on the end of the dock, and so she did not reply. She remained standing behind him, watching the moon's reflection weaving in a long uneven column upon the lake's surface, ending where Kale's feet splashed in the water.

"When we leave tomorrow," he said, "we'd like to take Amanda to Minneapolis for the weekend. We discussed it with her tonight, and she's willing."

She did not reply, for his words clogged her throat. They were taking Amanda away. She would be left with no one.

"You're also invited," he added. When she didn't immediately reply, he continued. "We wanted to wait until you were here to discuss it, but it got too late."

"It's going to be a busy weekend," she said finally. "I have to be here."

What would she do in Minneapolis? Sit and watch the Nobles get attached to Amanda? Listen to their plans for the future? Watch Kale ignore her? Even if it hadn't been a busy weekend for her business, she couldn't have gone.

"School starts in two weeks," she added, dreading what other plans they might have made for Amanda while she had been tending to her business.

He paused, and then replied, "She wants to stay in school here."

Jessi inhaled deeply and flung her head back in relief and gratitude. The sky's immense carpet of stars seemed to beckon when she opened her eyes, and she felt a stirring of hope that maybe things wouldn't be so bad. Not if Amanda wanted to stay in Kenross to go to school, and no one seemed to be objecting.

Or were they objecting?

"But will she?" she asked guardedly.

"If that's what she wants," he replied.

She didn't want to tell him how relieved she was, for their relationship was tenuous, and she didn't know how he would interpret what she expressed, and so she said nothing.

"That should make you happy," he said.

"Yes, it does," she admitted warily. "I wonder how long it will last."

"We wanted you to be in on the conversation tonight, but you were off somewhere," he explained.

"Medical transport to Duluth," she murmured.

"We all agreed that Amanda is mature enough to decide where she wants to live, and we warned her that none of us would condone her changing her mind in mid-year, whatever her decision," he said. "We aren't trying to take her away from here, but there are educational opportunities in the city—"

So, she had Amanda until June, at least.

"I heard you come back in the chopper," he whispered, abruptly changing the subject.

"I hope it didn't wake everyone."

"I was waiting for you, Jessi. I couldn't sleep until I knew you had brought your mercy ship home safely."

His words astonished her. "Thank you," she replied. But she had been back for at least an hour and he was still sitting here.

He rose from the dock and stood close to her. She stepped back from him, and then swung around and walked to the beach, squatting briefly en route to pick up her discarded shoes.

When she rose, he was standing alongside her, gazing toward the gazebo. "So you're going to sleep...there," he said softly. Was he letting her know what they had experienced *there* was already history?

Well, if he could be cool about it, so could she. "Amanda offered to keep me company, you know, but she slept there with a friend a few years ago and both of them came rushing back to the house in a panic before midnight."

"I suppose it can be a frightening place," he muttered, "stuck back there in the woods."

She felt the tears burning in her throat at the tenor of his voice, at the way he spoke of what was now a kind of love shrine for her. She heard him detaching from it.

"It has never frightened me. And I like the night sounds in the woods."

For a few moments he was silent, and then he said, "I know."

"City boy," she chided to hide the deep, sharp pain. "You probably never heard all that chirping and screeching before."

"There were other things on my mind," he replied very softly.

She was melting, hungering for him to touch her, but pulled herself back. It was over. Finished. This was the man intent upon taking Amanda away from her. What had been magnificent lovemaking to her was probably not worth a second thought to him. They were still adversaries, and no longer lovers.

It was over.

It had to remain over.

"Good night, Kale," she said, pressing her eyes closed, part of her desperate to have him take her in his arms, part of her afraid he wouldn't leave.

She waited while he made up his mind, for it took long moments. Finally, he bid, "Good night, Jessi," and walked away toward the parking lot, and presumably his motel on the road beyond.

She slept alone in the gazebo. And remembered.

But it was just a gazebo again.

The following morning, she rose early and gave in to Regina's insistence she wanted to prepare one of her old-fashioned Saturday morning breakfasts that her boys and the Caldwell girls had enjoyed so much.

"But it's only Friday," Amanda declared.

"Shhh, don't tell anyone," Regina whispered, searching through Jessi's cupboards while Jessi leaned against the refrigerator and sipped her coffee, grinning.

A knock sounded at the door and suddenly Kale and Phil filled her small cabin.

She was aware every minute of exactly where Kale was standing, or sitting, and what he was saying, which was little as his mother and Amanda chatted, and Amanda responded eagerly to Regina's requests for spatula, frying pan, flatware.

After breakfast they ambled to the airfield.

Amanda was leaving her, flying to Minneapolis with Kale

and her grandparents to spend a few days because her computer class had ended and her regular school didn't start until after Labor Day. She didn't want to move to Minneapolis, Amanda assured Jessi, as if sensing her aunt's fears that she might not want to stay in Kenross once she had tasted the metropolitan flavor and the devoted attention of the Nobles.

She didn't want to leave her friends and her school, Amanda said. She only intended to visit.

Before Regina boarded the plane, she deliberately pulled Jessi aside. "Tell me what's bothering you," she said thoughtfully. "Are you afraid of losing Amanda? Do you think we want to keep her from you? What's wrong?"

"I think everything will work out just fine," she said, but when she looked into the older woman's wrinkle-framed eyes, she wanted to cry because she knew that Regina had suffered severe loss herself and she recognized the signs.

"Is it Kale?" Regina asked warily. "Did something happen between you two?"

Jessi sucked in a deep breath involuntarily and knew in that instant she had given herself away. She covered her face with her hands, but Regina reached up and pulled them down and grasped them. "What has he done to you?"

"He took me to paradise," she said shakily. "But I'm back now."

Regina winced and clasped tighter around her fingers. "I'm sorry, dear. Truly I am. He does that to women, but it never lasts. I don't know what he's looking for. I'm sorry it was you."

"That doesn't make me feel any better, Reggie Mom," she told her, barely holding back tears.

"I know. I know." Regina swept her into a warm, solid embrace and held her close for several moments. "Sometimes I'm sorry I can no longer control what he does." The older woman pulled away and cupped Jessi's face. "Find yourself a good man, Jessi. You deserve one," she advised.

Jessi had thought she had one, for a week. But he had been the *wrong* one.

When they were all gone, she checked the charter schedule and told Chaz she wanted to take the three-day fishing trip into Canada.

He was surprised, but he seemed to understand. "Time to get away for a while?"

She nodded. Yes, it certainly was, although she knew nowhere would be far enough.

Fourteen

Jessi returned from the fishing trip on Monday to find a message from Regina to pick up Amanda the next day at Crystal Airport in the Twin Cities.

Amanda and Regina were waiting for her, and she was touched to see that Amanda gave her grandmother a hug before eagerly stowing her bags. Amanda knew Jessi would let her fly the plane home. The passenger seat would become the instructor's position.

"It has been a lovely weekend," Regina said. "It's amazing, truly, the vitality she has brought into our lives in just this short time."

"How is Matthew?" Jessi inquired.

"Better," she said guardedly, nodding. And then she winced. "A little better," she amended.

"He has a place in the basement like a, uh, like an altar," Amanda said. "It's just pictures of my—of their son, Paul." Suddenly Amanda's head swung around toward the runway. "Wow! Look, Jessi, look at that Lear!"

Jessi swung around and exchanged opinions with her niece. They dreamed of someday having a small jet of their own, but it was more a fantasy than a plan. When Jessi turned back to Regina, the older woman was grinning and shaking her head. "You two are hopeless," she said, laughing. "I thought young women were supposed to like clothes, boys and rock music."

"Oh, we like those things, too," Amanda quipped. "But mostly we like aviation. It's where our future is."

"I suppose on your sixteenth birthday, we'll all have to come and watch you solo," Regina said. In an aside to Jessi, she winked and revealed, "We found out this weekend that age sixteen is magical for aspiring young pilots."

"Count on it," Amanda replied, her eyes following a small plane landing. "If we have weather, I'll just die," Amanda added. "Hey, Jessi, look at that plane, no flaps and landing halfway down the runway."

"Must be a student," Jessi replied.

"Yeah."

"I'm very proud of my granddaughter," Regina said, watching her fondly. "She reminds me so much of you, Jessi, when you were a girl. You've done a wonderful job with her. I hope she grows up in your image."

"Thank you," Jessi murmured. How could she feel resentful of losing Amanda when it was to Reggie Mom, whom she loved?

They both watched as Amanda crawled onto the wing and nestled happily in the pilot's seat. When Reggie Mom raised her eyebrows in question, Jessi told her both sides had controls.

They exchanged an embrace, but when Jessi would have turned away to board the plane, Regina was clinging to her arm. "One other thing," she said hesitantly, "I think I was wrong in what I told you about Kale. You aren't just another woman in his life. I think you're important to him in a very special way."

Jessi's face smiled, but her vision clouded as her heart

raced. Was this to be the pattern of her life now? First a downer and then an upper and then another downer. It was like plucking petals from a daisy. And every time Kale's name was mentioned, she felt a lump in her chest.

On the ride home, Amanda talked about exploring the house Kale and Paul had grown up in, and making as good a study as she could of the house next door where her mother and Jessi had lived.

"Their house is really, really big. I mean humongous," Amanda reported. "So is the one that was yours. Were all of you rich?"

"Houses were less expensive in those days," Jessi replied, not adding that both families had had more of almost everything than most people had, although they hadn't been what she would call wealthy. Both fathers had been successful business owners, Matthew with his engineering firm, Brad Caldwell with his three discount furniture warehouses.

"Kale took me to see where he works. Did you know he's actually in charge of the whole business? He showed me the CAD—you know the Computer Assisted Design thing—and some other three dimensional things they use for designing. He knows about other kinds of engineering, too. He's really smart, Jessi, and did you know there's a program for people who want to study aeronautical engineering? Doesn't that sound neat? When I get older, Kale's going to show me more about it. He said I should take lots of math and computer courses, and when I'm in high school I should take all the hardest science classes, like physics. I don't even know what physics is. He said I could call you from there if I wanted, and so I called the cottage, but there was no answer. When I called the field, Chaz said you took the fishing charter to Canada. Kale asked me all kinds of questions about you. I don't know what his problem was. He was kind of uptight about something."

"Oh?"

Amanda shrugged. "He took us to a nice place for dinner and I had the biggest hamburger I ever saw in my life. I couldn't finish it all. And then we got a movie and he came to Reggie Mom's, but that lady engineer kept calling him and finally he left."

"Lady engineer?"

"Yeah, somebody who used to work for him."

"*Used* to work for him?"

"Yeah, I guess she wants her job back or something."

It was dark when they landed, and the base was closed, but the runway lights were on, and Amanda helped her put the plane away. They walked to the cottage arm in arm. "I missed you," she told her niece.

"You weren't even here."

"I missed you anyway."

"Well, better get used to it, Jessi, I'll probably be going to Minneapolis a lot. I had a really good time. And there are some kids my age across the street. I mean, this will be home and that will be kind of like a second home."

Jessi noticed that Amanda still avoided calling the Nobles grandparents or calling Paul her father. "There are many advantages to being in Minneapolis," Jessi said reluctantly. "Maybe the Nobles would like to have you live there and—"

Amanda stopped abruptly and looked up at Jessi's face. "Oh, but they can't just do that, can they? Make me go and live with them?"

She gathered Amanda against her. "I don't think anybody will force you into anything, Amanda. We all love you too much. We want you to do what makes you happy."

"Well, I hope you won't let them take me away from you."

It was heartening that Amanda wanted to stay close to her. "Not if you want to stay here," Jessi assured her.

She wondered, though, if she would have the heart to fight the Nobles if they enticed Amanda to try the suburban schools near their house. The lure of the metropolitan Twin Cities with all their parks and recreation programs and festivals, the skyway shopping, the Science Museum, the Mall of America, was going to be tempting to a kid from Up North country.

Was Jessi destined, eventually, to lose all the people she loved?

Two weeks later, in early September, the Caldwells made a rare phone call to Jessi from California, halfheartedly apologizing for procrastinating on their summer visit until too late.

She told her parents about getting reacquainted with the Nobles and that Amanda was spending most weekends with them. Her mother gasped. Her father let loose familiar expletives.

"It's all right. Everything's cool," she said. "See you next summer?"

"We'll talk," her mother said, and Jessi heard sadness and reluctance in her mother's voice.

Strange, Jessi thought later, that she felt closer to Reggie Mom than she did to the woman who had given birth to her. She loved her own mother and worried about the consequences of her parents' obsession with erasing the past.

There had been something encouraging in her mother's voice, though.

"Grandma and Grandpa Caldwell won't be coming this fall," she said to Amanda, who was silent for a moment, biting her lip.

"I kinda knew that." Jessi watched her deny the disappointment she obviously felt. Amanda held up a red sweater over her open suitcase. "Should I take this? It's kinda heavy."

Jessi smiled. "It's probably too warm, but Reggie Mom loves red."

"That's because Grandpa likes it, I think. She's always trying to get him to notice things."

"Is he the same as when you first met him?" Jessi probed warily.

Amanda twisted her face and tilted her head in thought. "May—be," she said, dragging the word to two long syllables.

"He talks about his son Paul a lot, and he seems to forget he has Kale, who's alive."

"Does he talk to you?"

"Yeah. Sometimes. He calls me Jessi." She bounced down on the bed and laughed. "Sometimes he tells me he wishes you loved Paul instead of Kale. I don't think he liked my mom too much."

Jessi inhaled deeply and squinted at her niece, deciding to answer in the generic. "Well, not everybody likes everybody, you know."

"Sometimes he knows who I am, though, and he hugs me, and then he tells Reggie Mom, 'isn't she something?' It's kind of embarrassing, but it makes Reggie Mom feel good, so I guess it's all right. I think I won't take the red sweater. It takes too much room and I have to pack my homework."

It was a Friday afternoon, and the Noble Engineering plane was waiting on the tarmac for Kale to return from the Point Six bridge. Waiting for Amanda, who would be joining Kale for the ride to Minneapolis.

"I'm always so anxious to go, and then on Sunday I'm anxious to come home. Why is that?" Amanda quizzed, zipping up the bag. "Are you sure I'm not really your daughter? I don't seem to have anything in common with anybody else." She lifted the bag and set it on the floor.

"I wish you were," Jessi said. "You're the closest thing to a daughter I'll ever have."

"And I don't like being away from you for very long," Amanda added, looking around her bedroom for something she might have forgotten.

Jessi liked the way their mother-daughter relationship was a given with Amanda. It caught in her chest, though, the overwhelming love she felt for this child.

Amanda stood with her weight on one leg and folded her arms across her chest in mock consternation. "Well, are you going to help or not?"

Jessi laughed and reached for the bag, but her laughter died when she caught a glimpse of herself in the mirror. Two weeks of tossing through the nights and passing on meals were not looking good on her.

"I suppose," she muttered, leading Amanda out of the room, carrying the bag.

"We're a little early. Kale won't be back for another hour."

Jessi swallowed hard. "Well, you'll be ready ahead of time."

"You always say that. And then you're never around when he comes. When was the last time you even said hello to him?"

Jessi closed her eyes while her pulse picked up, causing her temples to throb. She shrugged in answer. "He doesn't come to see me," she said finally. And anyway she looked deathly today.

"Well, maybe not, but I think he feels bad when you ignore him. You used to be so close. Well, at least for a while. Remember when he used to hug both of us?"

Did she remember! She remembered more than hugs. She remembered things so sweet, there weren't words to describe them. And it didn't require memory to recapture the feelings. They were still there, powerful and painful, every day of her life.

Not seeing him was the only way to avoid the unbearable roller-coaster of emotions. She couldn't have a friendship with him, or simply an affair, and those, obviously, were the only options. "This is right," she told herself daily. "Eventually it will get better."

As they crossed the parking lot, she saw that the rental car had been returned. Kale was back early. She wasn't aware that she had slowed her pace until Amanda coaxed. "Hurry, he's here already."

Amanda ran ahead to hug him. Jessi watched the two of them, and the sight of Kale was almost more than she could bear.

As Jessi neared, she stopped, set the bag down with relief,

and watched Kale focus on her, his dark eyes flashing with intensity, his harshly carved features registering like a beloved ghost from the past. She wanted to touch him. She wanted to curl up against him.

"Hi, Jessi," he said softly, studying her.

Amanda was backing slowly away toward the plane, her eyes darting with keen interest from one to the other and back. Jessi had a fleeting thought that Amanda might have deliberately "forgotten" just when Kale was planning to fly away.

Jessi wanted to greet him, but words stuck someplace before she spoke them, and so when she opened her mouth, nothing happened. He looked wonderful, maybe even magnificent, and she remembered immediately why she had been avoiding him. Seeing him now would likely set her back the two weeks she had been staying away from him, making her recovery that much more painful.

He turned his head to smile warmly at his niece and then locked an unreadable gaze on Jessi, who opened her arms to Amanda. "I suppose I should let this future pilot sit in front," he said, and Amanda nodded eagerly in exaggerated agreement while she hugged Jessi goodbye.

Jessi stepped away from them immediately, threw a weak wave at Kale and strode swiftly to the office where she rushed to the second floor to watch them leave. She watched Kale talking to Phil. She watched his every movement, his lips moving when he talked, his hands gesturing and handing Phil his briefcase, hands darkly tanned against a sliver of white shirt cuff.

While she watched, she tried to hold together the broken pieces. He was a virile man who needed a wife. And children.

She knew it would be like this, as if she were starved for the mere sight of him. She had even avoided communicating with him on the telephone. It hurt too much.

How shallow his affections must have been, she thought, that he could now be content to be merely friendly. It would be easier when his work was done. Too bad it was going to be several more months.

She buried her face in her hands.

Phil was ready. Amanda was ready. The plane was ready. All were waiting for him.

He swung from the plane and charged through the office door. "Where is she?" he demanded of Chaz, who looked bewildered but nodded toward her office. Kale took the steps two at a time. She was sitting at her desk, but she rose quickly when she saw him, and he noted her mouth open in astonishment. He was a little astonished himself, for in spite of all his arguing with himself, in spite of trying to decide whether he should follow her, he had acted on a visceral impulse. He knew he made a picture of panic with his black hair heaved around from the wind, his suit jacket open. He stopped abruptly when he saw her, his heart beating too rapidly, his throat obstructed.

He moved toward her slowly and took her face in his hands. She resisted, but he forced her to look at him while he studied her. She wasn't happy. There were patches of darkness circling her eyes, which were tinted with a suspicious redness, and she had lost weight. His breath caught in his throat and sharp points wiggled across his midsection.

Something was wrong.

"What is it, Jessi?" he asked as calmly as he could. Hell, it was the only opening he had to start a conversation with her. She didn't look sick, exactly, just kind of...worn.

She pulled away. "Everything is fine," she said, turning to the file cabinet, out of his reach. Except that he followed her.

"You've been avoiding me," he said from close behind her, making her jump and turn. "What's happening? Have I done something to offend? Are you all right?" She was backing away from him, clutching a folder against her chest as he advanced on her.

She was shaking her head. "Everything is fine. As if it's any of your business."

"My God, Jessi, don't tell me it's none of my business. What happens to you is very much my business." If she only knew, he thought, and then he added to cover his feelings. "Amanda's living with you."

She stiffened at his words and he knew he had hurt her once again. "All right, all right," he conceded. "I'm taking liberties with our friendship. But, Jessi, you're a part of the family now. I want to know what's wrong." Hell, he was lying through his teeth, and he hoped it didn't show. If she only knew! Good God, if she only knew.

"I'm not part of your family, Kale. I just happen to be your niece's aunt," she said quietly, setting aside his only weak claim to be involved in her life.

He stepped closer then and gave in to the overwhelming impulse to gather her into his arms. He tried to be as gentle as possible because there wasn't much he did that didn't offend her in some way. At first she resisted him, but within seconds she relaxed and her cheek rested against the front of his shirt. He held her there while his fingers combed through her hair. He bent down and lightly kissed the top of her head, knowing she wouldn't stay long in his arms.

Having her in his embrace was like coming home. He felt his breath coming ragged and uneven and he wanted to squeeze harder to keep her close.

All his unnecessary trips to the bridge in the last couple of weeks were worth it, just to hold her for these few moments. With her in his arms, he pondered why she despised him. He'd been willing to try anything to get her back, but she never allowed him an inch—or a full minute, for that matter. She avoided him in Kenross, and on the telephone.

He had tried to approach her before, and failed. He had known after their week together at the end of August that no one else would do, that he had to win her back somehow.

He tightened his hold when he felt her tremble. He felt her

fingers clawing at his shirt, and he reluctantly loosened his hold so that she could slip away from him. He searched her face and her body, studying her carefully. Her pants were baggy around the hips, and there was a gauntness about her neck and cheeks. He didn't like it.

Mostly, it was the despair in her eyes that disturbed him.

"Can I do anything?" he asked on impulse.

She closed her eyes and bit at her lip, and then she looked him in the eyes and responded. "Yes. Yes, you can. Don't come back, Kale. Stay out of my life," she declared, her voice hoarse but firm.

He stepped back as if shot, and felt himself wince. He wanted to ask "why?" but pride stopped him.

"There could be any number of reasons," she said, answering the question he wasn't going to let himself ask. "Maybe there's a new man in my life. Maybe I'm in love. Maybe I just don't want to deal with you anymore. It doesn't matter why. It's what I want."

She stepped back from him once, and again, and rested her hand on the file cabinet. He looked at her face, the fatigue and defeat in her eyes, the vulnerable beauty that tore at his heart, the inner strength that impressed and now rejected him.

He nodded shortly and forced himself to stillness. It was a time when he needed his armor, when his insides were seared and stinging, when he needed to keep himself intact and surviving, somehow.

"I see. Well, then, goodbye, Jessi," he said and swung around to escape down the stairs. He regretted that the words barely had a sound, but it was all he could manage. He took the steps at a run and left the building as if it were on fire.

As soon as he opened the door of the aircraft, he called to Phil, "Let's go!"

Amanda turned around and questioned him with her eyes. He pursed his lips, flinched, and shook his head. Amanda hadn't said much about his and Jessi's relationship, but he knew their estrangement was distressing her.

He pulled the papers out of his briefcase, giving himself the appearance of being busy and unapproachable. In truth, he didn't know what was on the papers and didn't care.

A light had gone out. The familiar darkness was consuming him, again.

By the time the plane landed he had resolved to get on with his life without her. To hell with her. He had a life to live. No one was indispensable, not even Jessi.

When he escorted Amanda into his parents' house and smelled good food and heard soft music and watched the three of them hugging, even his father, who sometimes responded to Amanda, he found himself asking to be excused from dinner even though it had been planned. He begged off with an overload of work and a full day on Saturday, and quickly turned away from that homeful of love.

It was what he had always wanted for his parents, to find hope and fulfillment. And for himself? What had he wanted for himself but business success, and eventually a family nestled in a lovely home on Lake Minnetonka, a wife and children. That was what he had wanted until one day last June when he stepped off his new corporate plane at a small airport in northern Minnesota and had seen a picture on the wall.

Nothing had been the same since.

He wondered if it was possible to fall *out* of love with a woman like Jessi. It didn't seem likely. Any other woman would be an inadequate substitute.

If he lived his life without her, everything would be a substitute. Could he live the rest of his life like that?

Jessi didn't want him. He had a life to live, and it was time to get started.

It was both infuriating and devastating that she might be involved with someone else, but it was also hardly believable, he thought. You didn't look as if you were sick and unhappy when you were in love. Unless the person you loved didn't love you back.

Unless the person you loved didn't love you back?

Dear God, was it possible that she loved *him?*

And thought he didn't love her?

But how could she not know how he felt?

Still, he had been careful to wear certain armor, and he had been deliberate in defining his feelings as lust, and later as friendship.

Hadn't she seen through that?

To know once and for all whether the dream was more than a dream, he would have to risk his pride and his heart.

And there was that one inevitable question to address head-on: did he want her even though there would be no children?

In recent years he had had vague notions of having a family some day, and in recent weeks the question had surfaced in his thoughts many times. The prospect of never having a child with Jessi was overshadowed by the dismal reality of living his life without her.

He knew he could never marry a woman just because she *would* give him children. He would marry for love, and the woman he had loved for as long as he could remember was Jessi. There was no other choice for him.

In effect, they already had a child and her name was Amanda.

Amanda was their gift, as much their child as any accident of biology. Amanda was just about perfect. Paul's daughter could be his own, and Paul, wherever his soul rested, would like that she was being raised a Noble in a family full of love.

If it wasn't too late.

Fifteen

Jessi lay on the couch, watching images on the television. Outside the breeze off the lake was sharp and cold, and even though her cottage was surrounded by evergreens, dried brown leaves flew loose and wild, rustling against the windows and skipping across the porch.

She rose sluggishly to put another split log on the fire in the smoky stone fireplace, and then she returned to the couch and let fatigue overtake her.

It was lethargy, she decided. Or maybe, depression.

She closed her eyes, felt tears on her cheeks and thought of Kale and their wondrous hours in the gazebo. She remembered all the details of touching and feeling, of loving so intensely there was nothing anywhere, ever, to equal its magnificence.

The tapping on the door at first startled her, but it seemed to be coming from the TV, and so she settled back on the pillow and covered her eyes with the back of her hand.

Once again drifting, she opened her eyes to find Kale Noble hunkering down alongside her, his black wool coat open, a

light scarf hanging around his neck. His straight black hair
was messed by the wind. His dark eyes were burning with a
fire that warmed her soul. He was frowning slightly and his
lips were parted.

She was aware first of how handsome he was, dark and
exotic and virile, the ivory scarf contrasting with his dark skin.
And then his eyes drew her, because they were soft in spite
of his frown, and there was something new in them, something
deep and, Lord above, she saw that it was fear!

There was *fear* in Kale Noble's eyes.

Her next conscious thought was that something had happened to Amanda.

She breathed her niece's name on a frightened exhalation,
but he shook his head and cupped a cool palm around her
cheek. "Amanda's fine. This isn't about Amanda," he said
softly.

He searched her face for a few moments while she tried to
gather her wits, and then he stood and shed the coat and scarf.
When he came back to her, he sat on the braided rug with one
knee up and rested his arm on it. She looked at his ivory cable-
stitched sweater and marveled at his broad chest and wide
shoulders. She could see a tiny cut healing on his jaw, a shaving nick. She could see the faint suggestion of shadow pressing
to darken his clean-shaven face.

Then she remembered that she could not allow him back
into her life, and she jumped to sit up, recalling that just yesterday she had told him she never wanted to see him again.
He smiled at her, tenderly but uneasily, and pressed her back
down with a hand on her shoulder.

"Stay," he whispered.

"What are you doing here?" she demanded. Yesterday afternoon she had told him to get out of her life. What new hurt
was he going to deal her?

"I've come to have it out with you, Jessi," he said with
quiet intensity. He flinched when he added, "I think this is
the kind of conversation you only have once in a lifetime."

He was going to say something painful. She just knew it. She felt his hand on her face once again.

"It's taken since last night for me to build up my courage for this, Jessi, and I'm admitting I'm terrified. I'm so terrified, I'm shaking," he said. He held up a hand to show her, but it looked pretty steady to her, not at all trembling, as she was, from her fingers down to her toes. She should just send him out the door, but he was touching her, and it was devastatingly bittersweet.

"I don't understand," she told him huskily.

"I know."

"Kale—"

"I have some things I want to tell you. I've been thinking about this all night. Hell, I've been thinking about this for months, since last June, and I've vacillated and made decisions and unmade them. And I've been confused and angry. Hurt. I've been deeply hurt. And for a while, in August, I was happier than I've ever been in my life. I've been on this emotional roller coaster with conflicting feelings blasting me from every dip and curve."

His voice was low and soft, and she listened, mesmerized and fearful, her heart aching. So he, too, had felt the roller coaster effect of their relationship and he didn't like it either. It was heaven to have him grasp her hand and rub his thumb absently over her knuckles as he spoke.

"I hated you, Jessi, for so many years. I hated you for tearing my heart out when we were kids, for not caring enough. I hated you as much as I hated your sister for what she did to Paul. I didn't understand how it was for you, trying to help Charlotte, trying to comfort your parents, trying to find a cure for a broken family and not being mature enough to realize no human being could ever do what you were trying to do.

"I know this, Jessi, because I was trying to do the same thing in my family, and I couldn't accomplish it either. I couldn't put things back together the way they were.

"The difference is that I had people to *blame* for our tragedy. I had Charlotte, and the following summer, after you left me, I had you."

She wondered where the conversation was leading; he was so intense, obviously committed to making a serious point. She couldn't resist reaching her hand over and brushing an errant strand off his forehead. He smiled weakly at her gesture. Was he taking pity on her because he was going to break her heart yet again?

"I thrived on my anger," he continued, rubbing his thumb over her knuckles. "I drew energy from it, especially when I visited my parents. And when, last June, I found you here comfortably owning a very prosperous and growing aviation center, I finally had a tangible, living target.

"The only problem was, anger and hate weren't the only feelings I carried with me. There was another one I didn't want to recognize, or admit, even though it was the strongest emotion of all. It was love, Jessi. I still loved you."

The words jolted her and she involuntarily squeezed his hand, and flicked her gaze to meet his. Past tense, she noticed. *Loved.*

"I knew I wanted you. And when we spent the week together in August...Jessi, you made me whole. You healed the torn edges of my soul. You put my heart back together.

"And then, you said things that made me believe I had been a fool to trust you, and my own feelings."

"I know. I regretted those words later," she told him.

"Since then, I've been about as lonely as a man can get." He looked down at the hand he held and she wrapped her fingers around his thumb. He looked up and found her eyes. "What I'm leading up to, what I came here to tell you, what I want you to believe, because it's so true, is that I love you, Jessi. I love you so much it's driving me crazy."

She gasped and raised herself up on an elbow. "You what?"

She saw him swallow hard. "I love you. I want you to marry me."

"Marry you?"

"I want you to love me. I thought maybe you did, during the week I was here, but then I was so damned enchanted, I'm not sure if you were giving me love or I was just hoping that's what it was."

"It was," she whispered. "Oh, it was."

"I want you to give me another chance. I want you to come back to me," he said softly. "I can't get out of your life without trying to win you back. Do you understand?"

"Are you sure, Kale? Truly sure about this? You'll never have a child with me, you know. Are you willing to accept that?"

"My darling Jessi, we already have all the child I want in Amanda. And if we change our minds about that, we'll just find our babies from less traditional sources."

She loved him all the more for that, if such a thing was possible.

"I hope this isn't a dream and I'm going to wake up to find everything the way it was before."

"Not this time," he promised. "This time we're going to make the dream come true."

She wasn't sure what he meant, and maybe later she would ask. She leaned over and pulled his head toward her. "Will you hold me, Kale, and kiss me? Will you tell me again that you love me? Will you tell me I heard right, that you want to be my husband?"

"All of it," he said, kissing her lightly, and then more deeply, giving and taking, moving over her, pressing her full length into the cushions.

Unreal and overwhelming as she found his declaration, she believed him, as she might believe a miracle when it happened before her eyes. The specter of long empty years ahead disintegrated in a second's flash. The nightmare of living the rest of her life without the man she loved shattered and eased away like smoke in the wind.

"I love you," she told him. "And I want to be with you forever."

They slid to the rag rug and slowly undressed each other, cherishing and adoring, glorying in their new discovery, exploring each other with infinite attention and sweet passion.

He took her once again to the pinnacle, held her there with loving tenderness and devotion and a kind of wonderful wild abandon, and coasted back with her, holding her tightly.

Afterward they lay before the fire, their bodies entangled.

He took her hand, pleated their fingers together, and said very softly in her ear, "I want to tell you about a dream I had...."

Epilogue

Jessi thought Amanda looked too beautiful and much too adult in her red floor-length velvet dress. She was the picture of innocent loveliness standing against the backdrop of noble firs, balsam pines and thousands of tiny Christmas lights, framed by the narrow doorway to the side of the altar.

"This is soooo beautiful," Amanda sighed, craning her head to peek down the aisle without being obvious to the people in the church. "But I never heard of having a wedding on Christmas Eve."

"I never did either," Jessi replied, leaning as far as she dared to get a view of familiar faces greeting one another over the pews.

"Nothing's ever normal in this family, is it?"

"What's not normal?"

"Like meeting all these relatives I never knew I had. Like you and Kale having such a short engagement? And after you were so mad at each other, I thought you were never going to get together again."

"We waited thirteen years. You think we're rushing into this?" she chided. "There's your second cousin Jeremy. He's nice-looking, isn't he?"

"Which one is he? They're all good-looking." Amanda tugged at Jessi's white lace sleeve and stepped back from the doorway. "I knew last August we should be a family. I just thought you guys were being pretty dumb about it."

Jessi grinned. She had an impulse to hug Amanda, but the veil and the lace of her wedding dress had been so carefully arranged, she didn't want to disturb anything. "We had a lot to work through, but we always loved each other."

"Yeah. And now I'll have a family again. It'll be great, the three of us being together. I'm so glad we can keep the cabin, and the airport, and Kale can still have his business here and we can live in both places. Chaz loves running the airport when you aren't there. Do you think Grandma and Grandpa Caldwell will move back to Minnesota?"

Jessi inhaled deeply, still incredulous about the way things had worked out. "They might," she murmured.

"Grandma Caldwell looks scared," Amanda said, leaning close, hushing her voice.

Jessi smiled and looked down the hallway to where her mother stood nervously clutching her purse. "Reggie Mom will handle that. She can take charge. She'll make everybody feel good. She could always do that." It wasn't like the old days exactly, but Regina had found a satisfying closure by embracing the future and letting go of the anger of the past.

"I can't believe how everybody is so happy. I mean, isn't it just awesome?"

She slid her arm around Amanda's shoulders and pulled her against her, wrinkles be damned. "It's definitely awesome."

Jessi was startled when strong hands suddenly gripped her waist. Not that she didn't know instantly who it was. "Kale, you aren't supposed to be in here!"

He guided her farther into the hallway, away from the people waiting for their wedding to begin, and spun her around, pulling her against him to kiss her lips. "We've overcome worse obstacles than a silly superstition," he mumbled against her mouth. "Besides, I brought someone who wants a preview. I thought…he needs to feel important…and be reminded that he's forgiven."

She knew what he meant even before her father rounded the corner into the hallway. "I love you," she whispered close to his ear before turning to her father.

"Kale, you'll crush the veil!" Regina cautioned from down the hall.

Kale laughed, let go of Jessi's waist and grasped her hand. He extended his arm to welcome his soon-to-be father-in-law. "Your dad wants to hug his daughter before she becomes a Noble," he said, laughing.

Jessi looked at her father, and thought how wrong she had been to think the last dozen years had been easy for him. She hadn't known how he suffered, until he willingly came to her at the Nobles' house and said he had been too full of pride to admit he was wrong. Crazy pride, he said, had kept him imprisoned and isolated, but now he was ending his sentence. Family was too important. So were old friends.

The ravages of his mistakes might never disappear from his face, but now he smiled, grasping her and Kale's hands so that they made a circle. She could see that he wanted to say something special to her before he escorted her down the aisle, but his jaw quivered and his lips trembled, and the words were choked by his overwhelming emotions.

That in itself, she thought, was a tribute to their future.

"I understand, Dad," she whispered to him. "Thank you."

He nodded eagerly, and blinked several times, an awkward smile emerging from his tremulous face.

From behind them came Reggie Mom and Kale's father, who was shaking his head, frowning in thought, focused on her father. "How'd it get so mixed up, Brad? How'd it get so mixed up? Look at this…Kale and Jessi finally getting married, and there's little Jessi already twelve years old. And you and me—'' he shook his head in mock consternation ''—gray hair already. When was the last time we played golf anyway?''

Jessi looked around at all of them crowded into the hallway, drawn together while the church organ and choir filled the building with carols. Scents of candle wax and pine drifted around them.

She grasped Kale's hand as tightly as he held hers. What a way to start their life together, in peace and harmony, filled with love, inseparable, living out the dream Kale had told her about, and without relying on the magic of turning back the clock.

She gazed from face to face, her parents, his parents, Amanda…and, most gloriously, Kale, who squeezed her hand and winked, his face alive with loving promises she believed in.

It seemed everyone's eyes were glistening, but maybe it was just a reflection of all the twinkling Christmas lights from the altar area and the softly touching Holy Night chorus.

Maybe it was just happiness sparkling in their eyes. Like lovely little flames flickering in each and every one of them.

Like the fire in her heart.

*　*　*　*　*

LINDSAY McKENNA
continues her heart-stopping series:

MORGAN'S MERCENARIES
III
THE HUNTERS

Coming in October 1999:
HUNTER'S PRIDE
Special Edition #1274

Devlin Hunter had a way with the ladies, but when it
came to his job as a mercenary, the brooding bachelor
worked alone. Then his latest assignment paired him up
with Kulani Dawson, a feisty beauty whose tender
vulnerabilities brought out his every protective instinct—
and chipped away at his proud vow never to fall in love....

Coming in January 2000:
THE UNTAMED HUNTER
Silhouette Desire #1262

Rock-solid Shep Hunter was unconquerable—until his
mission brought him face-to-face with Dr. Maggie Harper,
the woman who'd walked away from him years ago.
Now Shep struggled to keep strong-willed Maggie under
his command without giving up the steel-clad grip on
his heart....

Look for Inca's story when Lindsay McKenna continues
the MORGAN'S MERCENARIES series with a brand-new,
longer-length single title—coming in 2000!

Available at your favorite retail outlet.

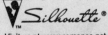

Start celebrating Silhouette's 20th anniversary
with these 4 special titles by
New York Times bestselling authors

Fire and Rain
by Elizabeth Lowell

King of the Castle
by Heather Graham Pozzessere

State Secrets
by Linda Lael Miller

Paint Me Rainbows
by Fern Michaels

On sale in December 1999

Plus, a special free book offer inside each title!

Available at your favorite retail outlet

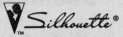

Silhouette ®

Visit us at www.romance.net

PSNYT

Celebrate Silhouette's 20th Anniversary

With beloved authors, exciting new miniseries and special keepsake collections, **plus** the chance to enter our 20th anniversary contest, in which one lucky reader wins the trip of a lifetime!

Take a look at who's celebrating with us:

DIANA PALMER

April 2000: SOLDIERS OF FORTUNE
May 2000 in Silhouette Romance: *Mercenary's Woman*

NORA ROBERTS

May 2000: IRISH HEARTS, the 2-in-1 keepsake collection
June 2000 in Special Edition: *Irish Rebel*

LINDA HOWARD

July 2000: MacKENZIE'S MISSION
August 2000 in Intimate Moments: *A Game of Chance*

ANNETTE BROADRICK

October 2000: a special keepsake collection, plus a brand-new title in
November 2000 in Desire

Available at your favorite retail outlet.